RESISTING
What's Real

KENZIE BRAYNE

HAVEN VALLEY HIGH #5
RESISTING
What's Real

MORLEY
BOOKS

Allie

I STRODE with purpose toward the three college guys huddled near the base of the stairs.

Ten. The voice on the radio began the countdown.

As I approached, Josh's gaze met mine, giving me the usual warm fuzzies. I closed the distance, weaving through party-goers until I reached my target. The two guys Josh was with also turned their attention to me.

Nine.

"I need someone to kiss at midnight," I told them, getting straight to the point. I was determined to start the year off right, and there was no time for small talk or introductions.

"What?" The guy standing directly in front of me dropped his mouth open.

I darted my eyes between all three guys. Josh had a slight look of concern that made my heart skip with excitement. If he was worried, he'd be more likely to volunteer. The guy on the right, the shorter one, was already fixated on my chest. Jerk. That ruled him out.

"I need someone to kiss at midnight," I repeated, letting my eyes settle on Josh.

Seven.

"I'll do it, sugar lips," the short jerk said.

I glanced over at him, then back to Josh, hoping he'd read something in my eyes and come to my rescue. But Josh stayed silent, maintaining the same concerned expression, only with his brow furrowing slightly deeper.

"Not a chance, bro," the first guy said. "She was asking me."

Five.

I flashed a smile at the first guy. He was well above average in the looks department—not that it really mattered—and at least he'd been looking at my face, which was always appreciated.

Was it enough?

I couldn't resist another quick glance at Josh. The first guy was above average, sure, but Josh was hot. Like, melt-a-glacier-in-five-seconds scorching hot.

With his chiseled bone structure, short, dark hair, and deep brown eyes, he could be on the cover of *sexy guys monthly*. Why wasn't his protective streak kicking in?

"Allie." Josh reached out to touch my arm, sending tingles through me. "You don't need to kiss someone at midnight."

Three.

"Yes, I do. It's good luck, and I fully intend to be lucky in love next year."

A slight scowl drifted over Josh's face, but then it vanished as quickly as it had appeared.

Two.

2

Josh shook his head, dropping his hand from my arm. My heart plummeted at the realization he wasn't going to step in.

"We doing this, or what?" the first guy asked.

My plan had backfired, but I'd power on. And right now, I needed that kiss. So I grabbed onto the first guy's shoulders and planted my puckered lips against his.

One.

A second later, cheers of 'Happy New Year!' rang through Mia and Josh's basement.

My mission complete, I moved to break apart, but the guy attached to my lips had other ideas. He opened his mouth, then brought his hand to the back of my head, gently holding me in place as he moved his lips over mine. He probed with his tongue, trying to get me to open up too.

It wasn't what I intended, but since I'd marched over and demanded to be kissed, I couldn't blame the guy for wanting something more satisfying. And I was painfully aware of Josh standing next to us. He had to be watching, and that thought was all it took to spur me on.

I wanted to make Josh jealous. I wanted him to pull us apart, to say I should be kissing him instead. Because tonight, for the first time, it felt like I had a real chance with my best friend's brother.

This was the start of what was going to be the best year of my life. There was a new optimism running through my veins, and I used it to fuel my kiss with this guy who tasted of beer and was doing an excellent job of devouring my face.

After what I figured was long enough, I pulled away from the sloppy kiss. But before I looked at the guy in front of me, there was something I needed to know. A quick glimpse to the side confirmed what I'd dreaded.

Josh was gone.

My kissing partner grinned. "Wow, that was the best thing to happen to me all year."

I laughed. "Me too."

So, he wasn't Josh, but he was cute, and funny, and although the kiss hadn't been great, we could work on that. He could still be the one to sweep me off my feet.

I tilted my head and gazed up at him. "I'm Allie. What's your name?"

"Chris. So, I take it you're superstitious, Allie?"

I painted a mischievous smile on my face and shrugged. "A little. But maybe I just wanted an excuse."

Chris's grin broadened. "I love it when a girl goes after what she wants."

He might say that, but in my experience, guys wanted to chase. Being forward never worked well for me in the past.

"I don't think I've seen you around campus, and I would've remembered." His eyes traveled over me in silent appraisal.

"I'm still in high school."

"A senior?"

I nodded.

Chris reached out to touch my hair, twisting the wavy blonde strands around his fingers. He was grinning as if he'd won some kind of prize. "So, how come you're here tonight? You like the older crowd?"

I was already eighteen, and from what I could tell, most people here were college freshmen. I doubted many of them were much older than I was.

"This is my best friend's house. I'd never miss one of her parties."

Everything was different tonight, though. Mia was in a brand-new relationship with Josh's best friend, Ryder, and they were going to be amazing together. I was doing my best not to crowd them, while also trying not to dwell on the fact that over the past few months my friends had all paired up and found love. I was the only single person left. The odd sock that no one wanted.

I wasn't a quitter though. I'd kiss as many frogs as it took. My perfect guy was out there, and he might be standing in front of me right now. I was willing to give anyone a chance.

Chris wound my hair tighter. "Your best friend's house, huh? Guess that means you're allowed upstairs? Want to show me around?"

He stilled his hand and gave me a confident smile. My pulse sped up in response. Then, as if I was incapable of reading between the lines, he leaned in and added, "Find somewhere private where we can get to know each other?"

2

Josh

MY EYES ZEROED in on Ryder's hands gripping Mia's hips. My instinct was to tear him off her, but I resisted, and the beaming smile on my sister's face told me it wasn't unwanted attention.

This would take some more getting used to, even though, as the two people I loved the most, I was happy for them. And I trusted Ryder. If Mia insisted on having a boyfriend, she was safest in his hands. His hands which looked like they were creeping lower...

I couldn't stop myself from interrupting. "Hey, guys. Happy New Year."

Ryder released Mia before turning to face me. "Happy New Year." He shared a knowing glance with Mia, then smiled at me with thinly veiled amusement in his green eyes. "Dare we ask if Allie found you?"

"Was she looking for me?"

Guess they'd heard about Allie wanting to ring in the new year with a kiss.

Mia scowled. "Don't play games, Josh. Just tell us what

happened." She sounded annoyed, but it was only out of concern for Allie.

I shrugged. "She advanced on us and demanded to be kissed."

Mia winced. "Tell me you didn't."

I held up my hands to display my innocence. "Of course not."

Not that I hadn't considered it. Damn, Allie was tempting. But I couldn't do it. She deserved so much better than me. Although, after watching Chris slobbering all over her, I wasn't convinced he was any good for her either.

"Did anyone kiss her?" Mia asked.

"Yeah, that guy Chris. The one with the shaggy hair." I turned to Ryder, thinking he might have more insight since I barely knew the guy. "They were really going for it."

I'd been willing her to push him away, but my mind-control abilities were lacking, and if that was what she wanted, there wasn't much I could do.

"I know who you mean," Ryder said, but his expression wasn't showing much approval.

"Well?" Mia looked at him with raised eyebrows. "What's he like?"

"I don't know him well, but I doubt he'll fit Allie's criteria for a *real boyfriend*."

"Is she still with him?" Mia asked me through her frown.

The last time I saw them, Chris had been playing with Allie's hair, but as I gazed toward where they'd been standing, they were nowhere to be found. "They were together a few minutes ago. Maybe you should go check if she's okay?"

I'd promised myself that this year I would relax, let people make their own mistakes, not interfere, or try to make anyone *off-limits* again. But I still couldn't bear to see Allie get hurt.

Mia nodded, then after reaching up to give Ryder a quick peck on the lips, she scurried away.

"Give it to me straight," I said.

"Total player. Worse than you." Ryder snickered.

I shook my head. "You're talking about the old me."

Ryder lifted his eyebrows. "Are you serious? You're planning to settle down?"

I scoffed, not sure what I was planning. I wasn't the type of guy who would end up in some lovey-dovey relationship. But I was tired of meaningless hook-ups. It was all so empty. "Forget about me. I want to know everything about Chris."

Ryder shrugged. "I haven't heard anything too bad." He frowned. "Are you actually worried about Allie?"

I tried not to be, but for someone so attractive, Allie was blissfully naive. Not all guys would have as much self-restraint as I managed around her, and I was scared one day she'd put herself in a situation outside of her control.

Ryder didn't wait for an answer. "I don't think Mia's going to find her."

I followed his eyes to where Mia was dancing in and out of the groups of people.

"Maybe they've gone upstairs," he said.

That had been the first thought to cross my mind when they'd disappeared, but I didn't want to believe it.

"Let's hope Allie remembers which door leads to her room and doesn't get the one next to it," Ryder continued.

I didn't want to fall for his teasing, but it was hard not to react. Allie was spending the night in the guest room next to my bedroom, and the thought of her ending up with Chris in my bed made me want to hurl. Or maybe just hurl something against the wall. But either way, I hated the idea.

"I expect you to remember the right door too," I said, lacing my voice with warning.

Ryder was staying with us over winter break. He'd needed a place to crash, and it was fun having him here, but that was before things changed with Mia.

He laughed. "I swear I'll stay in my own bed tonight. But if I get a visitor—"

"Ry." I slugged his shoulder. Not too hard, but hard enough that he stopped talking. "It's too soon for those kinds of jokes."

"Yeah, point taken." He rubbed where I'd punched, but the smile was still there.

"Did you just hit him?" Mia was back, and she sounded appalled.

"Just a reminder to behave."

She slinked over to Ryder, who wrapped his arm around her like there was some kind of magnetic pull, then kissed the top of her dark head of hair.

"I couldn't find Allie." Mia shrugged.

Was that it? She wasn't going to track Allie down? Make sure she was okay?

Mia studied me as if reading my mind. "You can't control who she dates."

"I'm not trying to control anything."

"Look, Josh. It's sweet that you're concerned, but just because you don't have to look out for me anymore, it doesn't mean you should transfer that energy onto Allie."

My jaw dropped. I didn't even know where to start with responding to that. I'd stop looking out for Mia at the same time I stopped breathing, and wanting to protect Allie was nothing new.

Mia hesitated, maybe remembering a conversation we'd had where I'd explained how some guys might see a girl like Allie. "You think the guy she's with might be a *scumbag*?"

Yeah, she was remembering, and a flash of concern passed over her face. I didn't react. It didn't sound like Chris was a bad guy, but there was a gnawing in the pit of my stomach. A sense of unease that I was struggling to ignore.

"I'm going to look for her upstairs," Mia said. She pointed a slender finger at me. "You stay here."

"No way."

"Yes, way. If you show up all uber-protective, it'll only make Allie's crush on you worse. Then she'll never get a real boyfriend. Is that what you want?"

I blew out my breath. Even though I was secretly flattered by Allie's crush on me, nothing would ever happen between us, and I made sure she knew it.

"No, that's not what I want," I answered. "Fine, I'll stay down here."

I didn't want to, but Mia could handle the situation, especially with Ryder by her side.

Besides, we were most likely overreacting. Allie would have taken Chris upstairs of her own accord. He'd be having the time of his life—lucky guy—even though there wasn't a chance in hell he deserved her.

3

Allie

"I'M ALREADY LOOKING FORWARD to tomorrow." Chris grinned while we made our way through Mia's house toward the front door.

Grinning seemed to be his favorite expression, and I enjoyed that he was so excitable.

"I'm looking forward to it too."

"You're sure you want me to leave?" He raised a hopeful eyebrow.

I couldn't blame the guy for trying, but I'd already explained I wanted to take things slow. I was waiting to be in love before I let things get too physical.

"Sorry." I gave him an apologetic smile.

"Tomorrow, then." Chris dipped his head to give me a lingering kiss that was a definite improvement over our first.

He pulled away, so I nodded, then watched as he slipped out of the house into the darkness. Tonight had gone well, all things considered, and I couldn't wait to share my news with Mia. I found her almost instantly, sneaking down the stairs, hand in hand with Ryder.

kenzie_brayne

"Allie!" Mia's brown eyes locked straight onto mine and she rushed over to meet me. "Are you okay? We've been looking everywhere for you."

"Is that what you were doing upstairs? Looking for me?" I laughed, not believing a word of it. If I were her, I'd have been all over my sexy new boyfriend.

"Actually, yes. When you disappeared with that Chris guy, we got worried."

"Worried? Why?"

Mia hesitated. "It's just that if you went upstairs with him, he might think you'd want to… and I knew you wouldn't… and then what if he…"

Mia trailed off, as if realizing how ridiculous she sounded. It wasn't as if guys wanting more was anything new. But she was worrying for nothing. No one had ever tried to force themselves on me.

"You know me better than that," I said. "I wouldn't go upstairs with someone I've only just met."

Guilt flashed over Mia's face. "Of course not. I shouldn't have listened to—I'm sorry. So where were you?"

"Out in the backyard." We'd caught the end of a neighbor's fireworks display, and it had been so pretty. I loved seeing the bright sparkles in the night sky. "Anyway, I have news."

"Good news?" Mia's eyes lit up. It was always so easy to read her emotions.

"Yep. I have a date tomorrow. Technically tonight."

Josh's voice came from behind me. "With Chris?"

I whipped around to face him.

"Are you sure about him, Allie?"

Before I could answer, Mia spoke up. "I thought you were waiting downstairs?"

"I was, but you were taking ages and now everyone's gone."

"Everyone's gone?" I repeated. Had I been with Chris for that long? "The party's over?"

"Yeah, there's a big street race going on, so they all rushed out," Josh said. "Anyway, I don't know about you guys, but I'm beat. See you all tomorrow for the big cleanup."

Cleaning up afterward was the worst thing about parties, but I would always stick around to help. It was miraculous how there never seemed to be anything broken, or anything too unsavory to mop up.

Josh moved toward the stairs, then glanced at Ryder. "Remember what I said."

Ryder let out a low chuckle, but he nodded. Josh's stern expression softened, and he turned away again, apparently satisfied with that response.

"Tell me about Chris, and your date plans." Mia raised her eyebrows, not hiding her excitement. She knew how much I wanted a boyfriend, and every new date was an opportunity. A chance to find love.

Josh hesitated on the first stair, and my heart skipped a beat. He wanted to hear about it too.

"It's just a casual date. We're only going to Jimmy's for burgers. Then maybe somewhere else afterward, but Chris is keeping that a surprise. Either way, it'll be low key."

Mia smiled. "Sounds perfect. You can talk, get to know each other."

"What?" Josh gawked at Mia. "You think going to some secret surprise location with a guy who's practically a stranger sounds perfect?"

It was a struggle not to read into the concern in his voice.

13

"They'll be starting off in public." Mia shrugged. "And if Allie doesn't like the sound of the surprise when he tells her, then she can come home." She turned to look at me, worry lines appearing on her forehead. "You'll call us if you need anything? If he makes you uncomfortable."

I nodded. It always baffled me the way everyone thought my dates would end in disaster. That I'd get myself into trouble and need rescuing. It was nice that they cared, but I was sure other people didn't get this same level of concern.

"I'll be fine," I told her in my most reassuring voice. "But I'll need energy, so I'd better get some sleep."

I followed Josh up the stairs and down the hallway to the left. He didn't say anything until we stopped outside the bedrooms.

"Be careful with Chris. He has a reputation."

I scoffed. "So do you, and I feel safe with you."

Josh frowned. "That's different. We've known each other forever, and we aren't going on a date."

I tilted my head. "So you're saying that if we *were* going on a date, I'd need to be careful?"

Josh broke out into a smile. The kind of smile that made my heart somersault. "You're putting words in my mouth. Besides, you know that'll never happen."

That stung. "Even now Mia and Ryder are together. Surely I'm not still off-limits?" I stepped closer to him and placed my hand on his arm.

Josh knew how I felt about him, and even though he was happy to flirt with me, he'd never allowed things to go further and had brushed off my many attempts at seduction.

But there was always something in the way he looked at me, something indescribable that made me not want to give

14

up. Something that made me think, despite his objections, that one day I might win him over.

Josh laughed and took a step back, opening the door to his bedroom. "You can do a lot better than me. And better than Chris, too."

I shook my head in frustration, but Josh just gave me a kind smile before disappearing into his room. He'd given that excuse before, but it made no sense. I didn't want better than Josh.

He was perfect boyfriend material.

But even though I didn't want to give up, deep down I kind of had. I'd long ago accepted that Josh didn't want the same as me, and if flirting like crazy over the summer hadn't been enough to change his mind, nothing would be.

And that was why I needed to focus on the future. A bright, shiny future that would begin tomorrow. With Chris.

4

Allie

I WAS in the middle of an awesome dream where Josh and Chris were dueling for my attention, proper medieval style, when my ringtone woke me.

Groaning, I reached out for my phone, but my muscle-memory proved useless and instead I grabbed air. My phone wasn't in the usual place, because *I* wasn't in the usual place.

I sat up in bed with reluctant half-open eyes, located my phone, then answered the call. It was Mom.

"Happy New Year," she told me. "Did I wake you?"

"Yeah. What time is it?"

It was still dark out. There was no way I'd had sufficient beauty sleep for my date.

"It's nearly seven. I need to go to work, but Gavin's tutor is coming this morning, and someone needs to be here to pay him, and to make sure Gavin is up and ready. And that he behaves."

I yawned. "Yeah, okay. Do you want me to come home right now?"

"Yes. As soon as possible."

I hated being in charge of rounding up Gavin, but it was me or nobody.

"Okay. See you soon."

I dragged myself out of bed, then threw on the same clothes I'd worn yesterday before the party. Mom wouldn't approve of that, but that's what she got for summoning me home in the middle of the night.

After gathering up the rest of my stuff, I went downstairs and out to my car, ignoring the twinge of guilt for sneaking out before helping with the cleanup. I fired off a quick message to Mia to explain, and I was sure she'd understand.

When I arrived home, Mom was in the kitchen, shuffling some paint swatches around on the table. She was wearing what she called her power suit, and she was exuding confidence.

She glanced up as I walked in. "Thanks, Allie. I don't know what I'd do without you."

"No worries."

"How was the party?"

"It was a lot of fun."

I lived for Mia's parties, although I preferred the smaller gatherings where there was more chance of getting a game of truth or dare going. They were always the best, and I loved the rush of adrenaline. The excitement of not knowing whether things would get wild. Never knowing exactly what would happen.

"So, any plans for this year?"

I laughed. "I still have the same plan from last year."

Mom looked up at me with one sculpted eyebrow higher than the other. "You don't mean the boyfriend thing?"

"Yep."

She sighed. "That's all well and good, but what about other hobbies?"

Other hobbies? Besides being dragged around the mall on Mia's shopping expeditions, my hobbies were basic. I liked the normal things. Bit of TV, bit of music, not too much sport, unless it was watching fit guys run around. Mostly all I wanted was to hang with my friends, laugh, and of course, fall in love.

I guess that wasn't enough for Mom.

"You think I'm boring?"

"Of course not. I just want you to broaden your horizons. There's more to life than finding a boyfriend."

I huffed. That was easy for Mom to say. She had no shortage of men tripping over themselves to get to her. And while I'd inherited her silky blonde hair, and her curves, I didn't have the same luck in love. Most of the guys who were interested in me were only out to cop a feel.

My prince was out there, though, and I was determined to find him.

"Just something to think about." Mom gave me a hopeful smile. "So, Noah will be here at eight for the first tutoring session. Can you let him in, offer him a drink, make sure he's comfortable and has everything he needs?"

I nodded. I knew how to look after a guest.

"I went to wake Gavin after I called you, but he got home late and was a tad grumpy, so I left him to snooze for a little longer."

I resisted the urge to remind Mom that my sixteen-year-old brother wasn't the boss of the family.

Or at least that he shouldn't be.

"Can you make sure he's up in time?" she asked.

"Sure." I could handle Gavin.

"Thank you, and here's the money for Noah." She handed me a wad of cash, then gathered up her swatches in one swift motion. "Guess we'll all need an early night tonight?"

Mom had been out with the girls. She didn't look at all tired, but she was always good at hiding her fatigue.

"Actually, I have a date tonight."

"A date? Who with?"

"His name's Chris. He goes to college with Josh."

Mom didn't look too thrilled about that. "Well, so long as he has Josh's seal of approval, I guess it's okay. But be careful."

"I promise."

Mom flashed me a smile before leaving the kitchen.

I wanted breakfast, but not knowing how long it would take to rouse Gavin, food would have to wait.

Upstairs, I knocked on his bedroom door, then waited for him to answer. Walking in on him, er, with his hands full, was not an experience either of us ever wanted to repeat.

"Go away." His voice was loud, but muffled, as if he was calling out while his face was buried in a pillow.

"I'm about to come in," I said. After waiting three seconds, I opened the door and stepped inside his room, which had the unfortunate stench of teenage boy.

Gavin was lying facedown in bed, and he chose to ignore my intrusion. I went to the window where I let in the light, then pushed it open to allow some fresh air in, too.

"Go away, Allie," Gavin mumbled. "I have a headache, and I'm not getting up for tutoring."

I sighed. He was going to be difficult. "Were you drinking last night? Get up. Your tutor will be here soon, and you can't miss your first session."

Gavin flipped over, revealing bloodshot eyes. "Last night

19

was wild. I regret nothing." He let out a parched, raucous laugh.

This was worse than expected.

"Stand up. I need to check you for tattoos."

Gavin laughed again. "I don't remember getting any, but who knows... and I'm staying in bed. Cancel the tutor."

He flipped back over, as if to signal the end of the conversation, but that wouldn't wash with me.

I put on my sternest voice. "You need to get up."

"Get lost."

"Mom put me in charge. You need to get yourself out of bed and ready for tutoring. Right now."

"Or else what? You can't do anything to me."

That sounded like a challenge, so I picked up his phone from the nightstand, then pulled his arm out from under the covers. I tugged on his arm, and he let out an annoyed groan.

"Give it up," he said. "You know you can't make me budge."

He was right. Despite the year and a half age gap, Gavin was already bigger and stronger than me. There was no way I could overpower him.

But that wasn't my plan.

I yanked on his arm again, letting him think I was trying to move him. Then, while holding his wrist, I positioned his phone in front of his thumb. As I pushed the device against his skin, the screen lit up.

Success.

Realizing what I'd done, Gavin swiped for his phone, but his reflexes were worse than usual, and I was quicker. I sprinted out of his room and down the stairs, narrowly avoiding tripping over my overnight bag that I'd dumped in the foyer.

Gavin stumbled after me. "Give it back! Or else!"

We ended up on either side of the kitchen table. I was safe. He couldn't get to me, and I'd successfully gotten him out of bed.

"Give it back, Allie," he said with a snarl. "My phone's private."

"Oh really? What's on here?" I thumbed at the screen, mostly to make sure it didn't lock me out.

The rage was building on his face. There was definitely something he didn't want me to see.

"Where should I start? How about photos? Or messages?" I pretended to be riveted, even though I was looking at the home screen. "Maybe I should take a look at your browsing history?"

"Don't you dare."

I pursed my lips and acted as if I were considering my options. I'd never deliberately invade his privacy, and if he stopped to think about it, he'd know that. Besides, the thought of what I might find was a powerful deterrent.

"I'll make you a deal," I said. "Go and get dressed, and you can have your phone back after tutoring. I swear I won't look at anything."

He scowled at me, but he knew I'd won. Plus, he was awake now, so he'd be more likely to stay up. "Fine. I'll go to tutoring, but I want my phone back right now."

"Hmm. You promise to cooperate?"

"I promise." He extended his hand toward me over the table, his face morphing into an almost angelic expression of hope.

I passed his phone over, and Gavin's smile broke out in obvious relief that I'd only been looking at a list of apps.

"Get dressed then. Noah will be here soon."

Gavin stomped out of the kitchen and up the stairs without saying anything else. Satisfaction filled me, but I only had a few seconds to enjoy my achievement before there was a knock on the front door.

It was Noah, ten minutes early. He gawked at me, as if the door swinging open in front of him was a complete surprise. I'd seen Noah around school, but we didn't hang in the same circles.

"Hi, Noah. I'm Allie. Come on in."

He didn't react at all, so I let my eyes study him. Clean-cut, with round Harry Potter glasses, he was casually dressed but seemed on edge. Like he was anxious.

Although, standing in front of him now, looking at him up close for the first time, I realized he was a Clark Kent.

Underneath the nerdy facade, he was cute, way more attractive than anyone would have expected, and I was hit with a sudden urge to give him a makeover. At the very least make him comb his black hair a different way. Or even better, not at all.

"You're here to tutor Gavin, right?" I asked, and that was enough to break Noah from his daze.

"Yes, er, hi."

"Come on in." I gave him a friendly smile, hoping to put him at ease. Then I stepped aside and gestured for him to enter the house. "I'm Allie," I repeated, not convinced he'd heard anything I said the first time.

He nodded. "We go to the same school."

"Right. Gavin's still getting dressed, but I'll try to entertain you until he's ready."

I beamed my smile at him again, and Noah returned it with his own nervous one. He really was cute, and something inside of me was dying to flirt with him, but I was wary of making him any more uncomfortable. "Come on through to the kitchen."

He followed me.

"This is the best place for you to work." I pointed at the table, and Noah placed his backpack down on it. "Can I get you a drink?"

He shook his head. "I'm fine, thanks."

Noah began to unpack his bag.

"Gavin shouldn't be too long," I said, not wanting to wait in uncomfortable silence. "So, you do a lot of tutoring?"

"Mostly physics. Same as your friend Chloe." He looked up at me, so I nodded. Chloe was making a killing as a physics tutor. "This is my first time with English lit."

"Branching out. Is that because Chloe's stealing all your customers?"

He smiled. "There are more than enough to go around, but they asked me to give English a try, so…" He shrugged. "Tutoring's a job, but, er, I guess it's sort of a hobby too." He adjusted his glasses.

"What other hobbies do you have?" I wasn't about to take up tutoring, but Mom had a point. I needed something else fun to focus on other than boys.

Noah's eyes widened at my question. "Um, I have a lot. I like to stay busy, but I guess tabletop gaming is my favorite. At least that's where my tutoring money disappears to."

Tabletop gaming? Was that as nerdy as it sounded? I was

about to ask him more when Gavin entered the kitchen carrying some books.

"Hey, man." He nodded at Noah, before slumping into a chair.

"Hello."

"I'll leave you boys to it," I said, wondering if they would even bother with introductions. "Let me know if you need anything. I'll be in the living room."

I grabbed an apple from the fruit bowl on my way out of the kitchen. It would have to do for breakfast until tutoring was over.

Gavin's grades had taken a tumble in recent months. Mom blamed some new *bad-influence* friends. But whatever the cause, I didn't want to get in the way.

I curled my legs under myself as I sat on the couch. Then I pulled out my phone for entertainment while I munched on my juicy red apple.

Mia had replied to my message.

MIA

No worries, we can manage cleanup. Good luck tonight! I'm expecting a full progress report

I smiled to myself. I always shared the details with Mia. She was my number one confidante, and she was also always ready to provide commiseration.

Hopefully tonight I wouldn't need any. Because I had a good feeling about Chris.

Tonight was a new beginning, and I intended to put in as much effort as needed so that nothing could go wrong.

5

Josh

THE HOUSE WAS quiet when I stumbled out of bed and went downstairs. Guess that meant Allie was still sleeping, because normally her laugh would fill the entire house, brighten whatever room she was in.

As I was about to enter the kitchen, I stalled in the doorway.

It looked like Ryder had made a start on breakfast, because there were mixing bowls out and already a sprinkling of flour on the island counter. That was a great thing, because his waffles were to die for.

Less great was the way he was kissing my sister and running his hands all over her back.

"Enough." I groaned.

They jerked apart, and Ryder at least had the decency to look guilty. "Sorry, bro, didn't hear you."

I shook my head in distaste as I dropped into a chair. "We're gonna need some ground rules."

Mia laughed, as if she thought I was deluded. But Ryder

was loyal. He wouldn't subject me to trauma-inducing sights if I asked him not to.

Proving me right, he answered, "Sure. We'll behave. Sorry."

Ryder returned to cooking, tipping even more flour into the mixing bowl, most of which puffed up into a cloud in the air. It would fall and settle, somehow all over the kitchen.

Without meaning to, I'd assigned myself the job of kitchen cleaner. And while I loved Ryder's cooking, I was less enthusiastic about the mess he left behind.

Mia studied my face. "Why do you look so grumpy this morning? You were more relaxed about us yesterday."

It was a fair question. One I didn't have an answer for. I woke up in a bad mood for no apparent reason. "I'm just tired."

"Did Allie's snoring keep you awake?" Mia let out an affectionate chuckle.

I shook my head with a smile. "You know I can sleep through anything."

I'd witnessed Allie's snoring one time when she fell asleep during a movie—some boring weepy drama. She'd made a lot of noise for someone so small. It was kind of endearing.

Mia furrowed her brow. "So, what's wrong?"

"Nothing's wrong except I'm ravenous." I shot a glance in Ryder's direction and he grinned, understanding my *hurry up* message loud and clear.

"You want some coffee?" Mia asked.

"Yeah, thanks."

I waited while Mia filled a mug then pushed it across the table toward me, earning herself a smile of gratitude.

"Drink up," she said. "We have lots to get done today."

"Like what?"

"The basement. Your friends left more mess than mine ever do."

That might have been true, but the bulk of the job was taking down the decorations. "It won't take long with four of us."

"Three. Allie had to go home."

"She already left?" My voice sounded more disappointed than I'd intended.

Mia nodded.

My mind remained blank while I drank my coffee and then feasted on Ryder's waffles, which Mia artfully decorated with fresh berries. After adding some extra syrup, they were heavenly perfection.

"So good." I took another mouthful. "You guys could open a restaurant."

Ryder never cooked like this at the dorms. He claimed it was due to lack of facilities, but I suspected his efforts here were to impress Mia. We'd be heading back in three days, and I was going to miss eating like a king.

After breakfast, I cleaned away the mess, then went down to join the others in the basement.

"Remind me why we don't call in the professionals," I said as I picked up another red plastic cup from the floor.

"The same reason we don't have a house cleaner. Because it's nothing we can't handle ourselves," Mia answered, as if that explained everything.

I was intending to argue back, but her ringing phone stole our attention.

She smiled as she checked the display. "It's Mom."

Our relationship with our parents had never been great.

They were *vacationers* and spent most of their time away from home. Not just physically, but mentally too. It was as if we failed to exist for them when they weren't in Haven Valley. Even when we were kids, we'd spent more time with a string of nannies than with them.

I was over it, but their absentee parenting style had been getting Mia down. So, when they came back for a fleeting visit over Christmas, I let them know how much Mia needed them. So far, things seemed to be improving. I shared a knowing smile with Ryder, who was equally happy for her.

"Happy New Year, Mom," Mia answered. "Yeah, it was just a few of Josh's college friends."

Ryder and I worked together to take down some of the higher up decorations, while I kept an ear on Mia's conversation. No surprise that Mom was doing most of the talking.

"Josh is here too," Mia said after a few minutes. "Do you want to tell him Happy New Year?"

I took a step toward her, but the way Mia's face fell stopped me in my tracks.

"Sure, I'll tell him," she said. "Thanks for calling—love you too, bye."

Mia ended the call, then gave me a sympathetic smile. "She had to go, but she says Happy New Year."

That figured. Why did I expect anything else?

I faked a smile. Even though Mia would understand how I felt better than anyone, I didn't want her to worry.

The only thing that mattered was that Mom was making an effort with Mia, not whether or not Mom thought I was worth twenty seconds of her time.

The rest of the cleanup went quickly. I stayed stuck inside my head, the disappointment from Mom's call lingering. I was such an idiot to get excited by any whiff of attention. Mom and Dad made no pretense of loving me.

"Good as new." Mia glanced around the room in satisfaction. Knowing her, she'd be planning another party for next weekend, and a whole new set of decorations would go up.

"Does that mean I'm free?" I asked.

My normal morning routine involved basketball practice with Ryder outside, but today we'd given in and agreed to help with the basement first. And now that Mia had a hold of him, I figured I'd lost Ryder for the rest of the day.

"Yes. You're dismissed. Thanks." Mia gave me a smile. A smile that said *please go away so I can be alone with my new boyfriend.*

I chuckled. I could play games with them. It was almost too easy, but ultimately, I didn't want to stand in the way of their relationship. I'd done that enough already. "Great. I'll head out then."

I wasn't entirely sure what to do with the rest of the afternoon, but I'd find a way to pass the time, and at least I had plans for tonight. I knew where I needed to be.

6

Josh

I WAS no stranger to bad ideas, but this one topped them all. I had no place being here.

"Can I get you anything else?"

I peered over the top of the menu to see my middle-aged server's slightly bemused face. She must've already thought I was a weirdo when I asked to keep hold of the menu after ordering, but that I'd held it in front of myself like a laminated shield for the past twenty minutes was suspicious behavior.

"I'm good, thanks." I shot her a smile, and from the way her expression changed, I could sense her warming to me. It was incredible how easy it was to get people to like you just from one look, even though it was only skin-deep.

"Let me know if you change your mind."

I nodded, and she left me in peace to get back to my spying. I mean my... what the hell was I doing?

I peeked around the side of the menu. Allie and Chris were still eating, and without warning, Allie broke into a fit of laughter. I scowled. Guess Chris was a comedic genius.

Allie tossed her head back, and when she straightened up

again, her eyes landed right on me. *Crap*. From the surprise on her face, this was the first time she'd noticed me. But I hadn't intended for her to see me at all.

I held Allie's gaze for a second before looking away, hiding behind my menu again. *What now?* I racked my brain for a plausible explanation why I might be here.

Less than a minute later, Allie slid into my booth, sitting opposite me and keeping her head ducked down low. "What are you doing here, Josh? Were you spying on me?"

I winced at her accusatory tone, but Allie wouldn't believe any of the poor excuses I'd thought up. I was here alone, and it was obvious why.

"Don't freak out. I only wanted to make sure things were under control. You weren't supposed to see me."

"So you're here as some kind of chaperone? Like a bodyguard?"

I'd been bracing myself for a bad reaction, but instead her light brown eyes lit up, highlighting their golden tints. I blew out a slow sigh of relief. I should've known Allie would like the idea of me protecting her.

"Thank you." She gave me a heart-melting smile, like it made her so happy to know I cared. But she already knew that. Didn't she?

"How's it going over there?" I asked. "You looked like you were having a good time."

"It's going great. Chris is so funny. He might be the one." She bit down on her lip and raised her eyebrows in an exaggerated display of excitement.

That should have made me happy, but the thought left me cold. I barely even knew the guy, but I'd already convinced myself that he wasn't good enough for her.

I gave Allie a smile of encouragement anyway. "Fingers crossed."

She craned her neck to glance back at Chris, and I forced my eyes to follow her gaze, even though they had a mind of their own and wanted to stay on her slender neck. Chris tapped away on his phone, and he had a smug smile.

Allie turned her pretty, heart-shaped face back to me. "It means a lot that you came here tonight. But you didn't need to hide from me."

"Yeah, I realize that now." I paused. "Do you want me to leave?"

Allie hesitated. "Actually, Chris was talking about going to a party at one of the warehouses off Spring Brook Road. You know where I mean?"

I nodded. Those were raves.

"He said it's up to me, and I want to say yes. I'm sure it's safe, but—"

"I'll follow you there."

Relief flashed across her face, and that was enough to put me on edge. If she genuinely thought it was safe, my presence would be more of an annoyance than a comfort.

"Thanks, Josh. Well, I should get back before Chris thinks I'm having bathroom issues."

"Sure." I laughed, then watched as Allie returned to her date, leaving me alone again.

I SAT IN MY CAR, drumming my fingers on the steering wheel. Leaving Jimmy's before Allie and Chris was a risk, but it would've been impossible to follow them here without being spotted.

So instead I drove out to Spring Brook Road and parked. My destination was obvious from the pounding bass and the throngs of people heading inside warehouse #3.

I waited until Allie and Chris arrived. Allie glanced around —looking for me?—while Chris led her toward the entrance. That was my cue to start tailing them.

The inside of the warehouse reeked. It was a pungent mix of sweat, alcohol, and perfume, along with occasional wafts of smoke. It was dark, but the bright disco lights and flashing strobes provided enough illumination. There were too many people here though. If I let Allie out of my sight, I might never find her again.

I kept my eyes trained on her as Chris led her over to the nearest wall. He placed his hand next to her head, then leaned in.

"Hey there," a petite girl, with purple streaks running through her short dark hair, called out over the loud dance music. She had a sexy smile, and from the way she was eying me, she liked what she saw.

I returned her smile. "Hey."

In a past life, I'd have been all over this situation, but remembering why I was here, I diverted my gaze back to Allie. Even though Chris was leaning in close, it looked like they were only talking—something it was too loud to do at a distance.

Purple Hair Girl stepped closer. "You wanna dance?"

Even though I was trying to behave this year, I was still only human and struggled with temptation. Turning down a hot girl was a huge test of willpower.

I sucked in a breath, then forced out the words. "I can't. I need to keep an eye on a friend."

Purple Girl followed my gaze as I looked back over at Allie and Chris. They were still only talking.

"A girlfriend?"

I shook my head. "My sister's friend. We think the guy she's with might be a creep."

Purple Girl's eyes filled with understanding, and some other emotion I couldn't name. It was possible she considered the idea that I was looking out for a friend to be some strange kind of aphrodisiac.

Chris pushed Allie against the wall. Even though it was clear what was about to happen, the way he dipped his head and plastered his lips against hers had me seething.

"Do you need to rescue her?" Purple Girl asked.

Did I? I wanted to stop what was happening, pull him off her, but there was nothing to suggest Allie was uncomfortable and wanted my interference.

What was I even doing here? Watching some lucky scumbag make out with her just on the off chance that he'd try to take advantage? Meanwhile, I had to suffer through it.

Chris so didn't deserve her.

He lifted his hand, then laid it to rest, right on top of Allie's left boob.

Damn. My breath caught in my throat, but before I could charge over, Allie pushed his hand away. *Good.* Chris let his arm drop, hanging limp at his side.

"Why don't you give me your number?" Purple Girl said. "Maybe we can dance together some other time?"

I tore my gaze away from Allie to look at Purple Girl. She

was sexy and giving me all the right signs. But I wasn't here for myself tonight. It was obvious my focus was elsewhere.

"Sure, I'd like that," I said, causing her to smile and pull her phone out from the little bag that was crossed over her body.

I turned my attention back to Allie, and this time, what I saw left no room for doubt.

Chris was a creep.

And I was going to stop him.

7

Allie

CHRIS'S LIPS formed a vacuum over mine. He kissed me with frenzied enthusiasm, and even though I'd pushed him away, after taking a quick breath, he came right back in for more. He was lapping and sucking, apparently attempting to reach my tonsils.

I was in way out of my depth.

Chris moved his hand back to my chest. I'd already brushed it off once, but this time, he took a firm hold, giving me a squeeze.

I grabbed his arm and pulled it back down so that he released me. He didn't fight the action, and a shot of relief hit me. I still had control. We were in a crowded place. He wouldn't try to take things too far here, would he?

I was safe. Right?

I didn't feel it. Instead, I felt like the biggest fool. Was I so desperate to find love that I'd take such stupid risks? Coming to a place like this with a virtual stranger. Why didn't I listen to the warnings?

Chris paused the kiss. "You have such amazing tits."

Before I could respond, his mouth was back on mine, and his hand returned to its favorite place too.

Stop.

I wanted to fight him off, but my body wasn't cooperating. His hand kneaded me through my sweater, and he pushed himself against me, pinning me to the wall.

I needed to stop him. Even if it caused a huge scene and I was left stranded.

No. I wouldn't be stranded. I could call Mia. She'd rescue me with Ryder. Or with Josh.

Josh.

He was supposed to be here, but I hadn't seen him since Jimmy's. There was no way he'd abandon me, but what if he'd lost me?

Or was he here? Watching now? What if he thought I wanted this?

I shook the thought away, unable to believe it. Josh was too protective not to interrupt something like this, even if he thought I was a willing participant.

Tears pricked at my eyes.

Josh isn't going to save you.

That meant only one thing. I would need to save myself, to face the embarrassment alone. There was no choice. I couldn't stand another second of Chris pawing at me.

Mustering up all my internal strength, I moved my hands to Chris's chest. Then, hoping that the internal strength would transfer to some external power too, I used every ounce of energy to give Chris a shove as hard as I could manage.

He flew off me. It was like there was no resistance at all.

"Hey!" Chris yelled. "What the hell, dude!"

My heart flipped at the sight in front of me.

I'd never seen Josh like this before. The rage was glowing in his eyes, and even though he'd let go of Chris after yanking him off me, Josh had balled his hands into tight fists.

Were they going to fight?

It wasn't the medieval duel I'd dreamed of, but my heart pounded from the sudden rush of adrenaline.

"Apologize." Josh glared at Chris.

"Relax. We were only having some fun." Chris looked at me with a bewildered expression, as if he thought Josh was completely overreacting.

Josh's gaze met mine, and I didn't have to say anything.

"She wasn't having fun." Josh took a step toward Chris.

Chris reacted by holding up his hands in surrender, almost cowering. "Alright, alright." He turned his attention to me. "Sorry, babe. I thought you were into it."

I frowned, then looked back at Josh, wishing he'd throw a punch.

"Don't you ever go near her again," Josh said, the dangerous warning in his voice unmistakable. "I mean it."

I loved that he wanted to protect me. And if there was a fight, Josh would win. He was strong, fit from playing basketball, and I knew he'd always stand up for me.

"Whatever. She's not worth the trouble." Chris glanced at me with a look of disdain. "You kiss like a fish."

What?

My jaw dropped, then realizing I probably looked like a fish too, I snapped my mouth closed.

Chris scowled. "Actually, more like a toad." He didn't wait for a reaction before stepping back and retreating into the crowd.

Was he telling the truth? Was I a terrible kisser? Was that why no one wanted to be my boyfriend?

Josh moved to stand in front of me. "You okay, A?" He took hold of my chin, tilting it upwards and studying my face.

I held my breath. Why did it feel like Josh was about to kiss me? He'd never do it, especially not right after what just happened. But there was something in his expression, like he cared for me deeply. And just seeing that look on his face meant so much that everything leading us to this point seemed worth it.

I nodded in his hand, letting the smile break across my face.

Josh saved me.

He bit down on his lower lip as if considering something, but then he released my face, and instead took hold of my hand, lacing his fingers through mine like it was such a natural thing to do. "Let's get out of here. I'll take you home."

Josh's hand was warm and strong. Safe. It was as if nothing bad could happen to me while he was attached. He led me toward the exit, past a stunning girl with purple hair who gave him a smile like she knew him, a smile that pierced me with a dart of jealousy.

Once outside, Josh kept a fast pace as he guided me to his car. He didn't say anything until we were both buckled in. Instead of starting the engine, he rested his elbows on the steering wheel and dropped his head into his hands. "Damn it, Allie. You know how that could've ended?"

He was mad at me?

"I—I know. I'm sorry."

He glanced over, his face full of frustration.

"I should have ended things at Jimmy's," I said. And it was

true. The alarm had sounded when Chris put his hand on my thigh under the table—way too high.

I hadn't been thinking clearly because my mind had been focused on Josh. I loved how he'd shown up on my date; that he'd sacrificed his evening in order to look out for me. But putting myself in potential danger? I was so stupid.

Josh let out a slow breath and then started the car.

"Thank you for saving me," I said.

"I'm glad I was there."

"Me too." I stared out the side window, ashamed of my actions. We rode in silence until I sighed. "I don't think I'll ever find a boyfriend."

Josh hesitated for a moment. "Of course you will."

I shook my head. "I've tried. There has to be something wrong with me. Maybe Chris is right and I kiss like a toad."

"What?" He blurted out a laugh. "No, I guarantee that's not it."

"I think it might be. There's definitely something wrong with me."

"There's nothing wrong with you, Allie. The problem is the guys you attract."

"What do you mean?"

He paused, as if unsure whether to continue. "I mean that guys look at you, and they think one thing."

"What do they think?"

Josh remained silent.

"Tell me, Josh. What do guys think when they look at me?"

8

Josh

HOW WAS I supposed to explain this? I glanced over to meet Allie's curious eyes.

"Please answer me. I really don't want to end up in a convent."

I couldn't hold back my snicker, and she smiled.

But the idea of Allie having more dates like this one, or worse, terrified me. Maybe telling the truth might help her. She could handle directness.

"Fine. They see you as a sex object."

"Seriously? You think?" She sounded more intrigued than offended.

"I know so."

If Allie knew the way some guys thought, she'd probably voluntarily check herself into the convent first thing tomorrow. And I couldn't even judge them, because, even though I was ashamed to admit it, I could be just as bad.

Allie had been best friends with Mia for years, so I knew her pretty well. I knew how sweet she was, and that she had a heart of gold. How she was kind and funny, always the life of the party. I loved the way her smile would always light up any room.

But despite all that, there were still times when it was a struggle to hold back my urges. Times when all I wanted was to grab hold of her and kiss her. And more. A whole lot more.

"Is that my fault?" Allie asked. "It's not like I dress slutty."

I raked my eyes over her clothes. She wore tight jeans and a tight sweater. There was hardly any skin on display, yet she was still showing all her amazing curves.

"No, but you have those." I let my gaze rest on her chest, then whipped my eyes away before my imagination kicked in.

"Are you being serious? My boobs are attached, Josh. It's not like I can take them off."

"I know that. I never said it was fair."

Allie huffed. "So I'm doomed."

"You're not doo—"

"But you're describing a stereotype, right? I refuse to believe all guys are that awful."

I cringed. "It's not all guys. But you need to attract the right kind. Find someone good enough for you."

I kept my eyes on the road but could feel her looking at me.

"How do I do that?"

"To start with, you need to tone down the sexy."

"How?"

That was a great question. Allie was drop-dead gorgeous, and just like she'd already pointed out, it wasn't really possible to hide her assets. But she was also a huge flirt.

Mia had let it slip that Allie was inexperienced, but she sure didn't come across that way with her confidence and fun go-getter attitude. It would be so easy for guys to get the wrong idea. To expect more from her.

"Will you help me?" Her hopeful voice interrupted my thoughts.

"Help you?"

Help her to be less sexy? To find a boyfriend?

"Yes. Help me attract the right kind of guy."

I glanced at Allie again. She was hell-bent on finding love. And even though it sent my jealousy soaring, I wanted her to be happy. I hated the thought that she might fall for some scumbag who didn't deserve her. He had to be worthy.

He had to be better than me.

This was a golden opportunity. A chance to guide her in the right direction.

I shot Allie a smile. "Yeah. I'll help you."

"You will?" She grinned, biting her lip.

"I'll try."

"Thank you!" She made an excited high-pitch noise, as if she expected me to be some incredible matchmaker about to make all her dreams come true.

"I can't promise you Prince Charming, but I'll do my best."

Allie nodded with enthusiasm. "What's the first step?"

"Why don't you tell me what you're looking for in a boyfriend?"

"Okay, well, he needs to be tall, dark, and handsome. Totally hot. Rich brown eyes. Athletic, but he doesn't have to be ripped. Not a slave to the gym. I want someone with brains, too. Being pretty isn't enough. Someone who knows how to take initiative. Good with his hands and with a great sense of humor. Most importantly, he needs to have a sensitive

43

soul, and be loyal, caring. Like he'd go to any lengths to protect his loved ones and keep them safe. You understand what I mean? Can you find me anyone like that?"

There was teasing in her voice, and it was obvious what she was doing, but still my heart flipped. Was that how she saw me?

"I'm not sure," I answered. "It'll be tough to find anyone that perfect."

Allie giggled. Her mood had changed so much over the past few minutes, and this was a vast improvement. It was as if she'd forgotten all about Chris, the creep, and was now bursting at the seams with excitement.

"Maybe you're right." She grinned. "In that case, I guess I'd just be happy with someone who treats me right. Someone I can have fun with. Who makes me feel loved."

"So long as he's still dashingly handsome?" I gave Allie a quick glance, winking as I met her pretty eyes.

"Actually, no. It doesn't matter what he looks like."

"It doesn't?"

That was so Allie. She was jaw-droppingly stunning, yet not at all shallow. It made my heart ache just imagining the way she'd look at her boyfriend—full of love and admiration, even if on the surface he was Quasimodo.

"Nope. I mean, of course I'd prefer it if he were cute, but personality trumps everything."

I nodded. That would make my job so much easier.

"How do I find a guy like that?" she asked.

Another great question. One I didn't have the answer to yet.

"Let me think about it. I'll come up with a plan."

Allie beamed at me. "I'm so excited."

Yeah, that was obvious.

"When can we start?" she asked. "When do you go back to college?"

"We leave Sunday night."

It was Friday, so we'd have most of the weekend. Plenty of time to figure it out.

"That's not much time," Allie said. "Are you free tomorrow? Can we get together in the morning? Mom wants me to stay home while Gavin has tutoring, but you could come over?" She hesitated. "Unless you already have plans?"

My only plan was to recreate an experiment I'd seen online which involved running a high voltage current through hot dogs, electrocuting them until they exploded. I enjoyed tinkering with electricity, but helping Allie was without doubt a better use of my time.

"I can come over."

Even once classes started up again, I figured I'd be back home more than usual. The dorms were only an hour away, and it was almost inevitable that Ryder would be back and forth to visit Mia. Unless there was a compelling reason to stay, I'd go with him, especially since he'd want to borrow my car.

"Thank you. I can't wait." She flashed me another excited smile. "You honestly think this will work? That you can help me get a dream boyfriend?"

I nodded. "We'll make it work. I promise I'll do whatever I can to find you your perfect guy."

9

Josh

"YOU CAME!" Allie grinned at my arrival the next morning. She wrapped her arms around my torso, giving me a quick hug.

I laughed. Guess her excitement hadn't faded at all overnight. "I'm always true to my word."

"Thank you so much for doing this, Josh." She stepped aside, gesturing with her arms that I should enter her home.

I'd seen the exterior of Allie's house on multiple occasions but had only been inside a handful of times.

"Let's wait for Gavin's tutor before we get started. Can I get you a drink?"

Loud footsteps stomping down the stairs drew my attention. Allie's brother looked as if he'd only just stumbled out of bed. He wore crumpled clothes and his light hair stuck up as if fully charged by static electrons. Gavin had been over to our house with Allie plenty of times over the years, so we were on friendly terms. I hadn't seen him since the summer though, and he must have shot up at least six inches.

He met my eyes and gave me a lazy smile. "Hey, man. I

thought you were Noah." He hesitated on the stairs, then glanced back up as if considering returning to his room.

"Don't even think about it," Allie said. "He'll be here any minute. Did you shower?"

Gavin scowled at her. "I'm fine." Then he looked back at me. "Are you here without Mia?" His face scrunched up in mild confusion.

I guess Mia was always around when I was with Allie, so me visiting her alone was odd.

"Josh is helping me with a project," Allie said before I had a chance to respond.

"What project?"

There was a knock on the door.

"That'll be Noah." Allie sounded relieved at the interruption.

Did she want to hide the reason I was here?

Gavin blew out a loud breath and reluctantly continued down the stairs while Allie answered the door.

"Hi," the tutor, Noah, said. "I'm here for tutoring again." He stared down at his feet, as if blinded by Allie's beauty. Like he was afraid to look at her.

Even as a spectator, I felt awkward on his behalf.

"Hi, Noah. Come on in." Allie gave him one of her warm smiles, and he glanced up, giving her a half-smile of his own before letting his eyes drift to me.

"Hey." I conjured up my friendliest expression, hoping it might put him at ease. It didn't seem to though, because he averted his gaze.

Allie grabbed hold of my arm. "I'll be upstairs with Josh. Holler if you need anything."

Upstairs? In her bedroom?

She pulled me toward the stairs before releasing me and practically bouncing up. I followed without words until we were inside her room and Allie shut the door behind us.

She sat down on the bed, pulling her legs up and folding them underneath her. Then she looked up at me with expectant eyes.

My heart pounded. We were alone in her bedroom—somewhere I never thought I'd be. And the way Allie was smiling at me, gazing with her beautiful light brown eyes, made me way too tempted to join her on the bed. Something I knew in my core was a very bad idea.

The worst thing was that she'd made no secret of the fact she was attracted to me. If I kissed her, I was confident she'd return the affection. I couldn't let that happen. It wouldn't be fair to her. I could resist.

Swallowing the lump in my throat, I leaned back against the door. I was here to help Allie. Not to act out my impulses. So, I tore my eyes away from her and glanced around the room.

It was tastefully decorated in lots of dull neutral colors with gold accents. The walls were bare, and it was boringly tidy. There was no personality here. Nothing about this room said 'Allie'. Nothing except for the giant stuffed giraffe that lay next to her on the bed.

I couldn't hold back the smile. "You kept the giraffe?"

I won him a couple of weeks ago on the Brookhill Christmas Carnival's ring toss game. I'd given him to Jennie, the unattainable girl I'd crushed on senior year of high school, but when she announced her intention to leave him behind, Allie stepped in to rescue the giraffe and had apparently given him a permanent home.

"Of course I did." She pulled him into her by his neck, then cuddled him in her arms.

"Does he have a name?"

"Of course he does."

"And…"

"Promise not to laugh."

"I promise."

She took in an audible deep breath before releasing it. "Mr. Giraffe."

I paused, my lips twitching. I'd expected her to say something humorous, but that was just… awful.

"Mr. Giraffe," I repeated. "Yeah. It suits him."

Allie laughed. "I know it isn't the most inspired name, but it was either that, or naming him after you. I mean, since you were the one to win him."

"Josh the giraffe," I mused. "I would have been flattered."

She shook her head as if she didn't believe me. Then, as if remembering why I was here, she jumped up off the bed. "Come into the closet with me. I want to show you something."

Her tone wasn't at all suggestive, but her words still had my mind jumping to various naughty scenarios.

Allie opened the door to her closet, then waited for me to push myself away from her bedroom door and join her.

At least I now knew where Allie was hiding the personality in her room. The large walk-in closet was a mess, with clothes strewn everywhere. There was a full-length mirror attached to the back wall, although I wasn't sure she could use it, considering the mosaic of photos and ticket stubs stuck on top of the glass. There was even a tatty old friendship bracelet attached.

Mia had one too, and the girls had worn them until they fell apart.

I walked over to investigate the mirror, my eyes drawn to a photo of Allie posing with Mia and their friend Chloe at Mia's last Halloween party. Mia was in her Black Swan ballerina costume, her dark hair wound in a bun, and Chloe was dressed up as Dorothy from the Wizard of Oz. But it was Allie who stole the limelight.

"Oh, that was from Halloween," she told me, as if I wouldn't have been able to guess. "What do you think of our costumes?"

Allie wore a black cat costume which clung to every perfect curve, and she looked incredible, something that was only boosted by the grin on her face and the sparkle in her eyes.

I'd considered returning home for the party, despite Mia's objections, but now I was glad I hadn't. It would've been a struggle to resist Allie if she'd flirted with me while looking like that.

I shook my head as I tapped on her picture. "This is too much. This is exactly how you'll attract guys for the wrong reason."

Allie pushed her lips to the side and bowed her head, as if she thought she was getting told off. "Well... in my defense, I *was* trying to attract someone that night."

"You were? What happened?"

She shrugged. "It doesn't matter. We weren't right for each other. I don't know what I was thinking. He's with Chloe now anyway, and I'm so, so happy for them."

"With Chloe? You're talking about Nate? You were trying to attract Nate?"

Out of Mia's friends, Nate was one of the most fun. I'd always liked him, so it didn't bother me when he got together with Allie last spring. Their relationship only lasted a few weeks, so I figured it was no big deal. This was the first I'd heard about her wanting him back.

Allie scrunched her nose. "That's ancient history, and besides, it didn't even work."

It didn't work? I gawked at her. Was Nate blind? Why'd he ever let her go?

"None of that matters anymore," she said. "There will be no more sexy outfits for me. Nope. I've already picked out my most dowdy clothes, and I wanted to get your approval."

"Dowdy?" I laughed.

"Yes. I don't have many, so I'll need to shop. But I'm sure Mia will help. You know what she's like when she's on a mission. I'm guessing baggy stuff would be best to hide my figure?"

She glanced at me, as if waiting for guidance.

I sighed. "You don't need to change your clothes."

"I don't? But I thought you said..." Her brow furrowed in confusion.

"You shouldn't have to change who you are. And you won't need to." I was going to find Allie the perfect boyfriend, and she wouldn't need to change a thing. "Because I have a plan."

10

Allie

THERE WAS SUCH a firm determination in Josh's expression, it was as if our quest to find me a decent boyfriend was already a guaranteed success story.

He had a plan, and I couldn't wait to hear it.

"Let's sit down," I said, leaving the closet and returning to my bed.

Josh followed me back into my room, but he didn't sit next to me, and instead he leaned back against the door where he'd stood earlier.

"What's the plan?" I asked.

He flashed me a confident grin. "Internet dating."

"Internet dating?" My smile dropped. Was he serious? That was the plan?

He nodded. "Hear me out. I'm not talking about setting up real-life dates on an app. I mean having the dates online. Staying anonymous. Getting to know each other without the distraction of outward appearances. You with me?"

I'd totally overestimated the help Josh would offer. I'd

expected some sort of insight into the male brain, something that could help me attract the right guy. This was the best he could come up with?

"You're suggesting I find a boyfriend in chat rooms?"

I forced away the feeling of defeat. Josh's plan might be a dud, but that didn't mean that *my* plan would be too. Because, while I was open to taking his advice and trying new tactics to snag a dream boyfriend, the entire time we were working together, it was bonus time with Josh.

It was impossible to push aside my feelings for him, and unless I fell head over heels for someone else, I didn't think I'd ever give up hope. Surely he had to relax his belief about siblings' friends being off-limits now that Mia and Ryder were together?

"It could work." The uncertainty in his voice made me wonder whether he'd only just thought up this plan.

"So, I'll talk to random strangers online?"

The exact thing the internet safety campaigns had convinced me never to do.

Josh studied my face then sighed. "You hate the idea. I just thought hiding what you looked like would be the best solution."

"Is my appearance really that big of a problem?" He made it sound like guys found me irresistible, but that clearly wasn't the case, because Josh managed to resist me just fine, even though I wished he wouldn't. "You don't think it's my personality? Or that I kiss like a toad?"

He laughed. "I already told you. There's no way you kiss like a toad. Chris only said that because he's a jerk. And don't worry, you have a great personality. Who wouldn't want a girlfriend that's fun and vivacious?" His smile went straight to my heart. "But it might be that you're too eager. Have you tried playing hard to get?"

"Yeah, I have. But nothing happens. If I don't approach guys, let them know I'm interested, they don't even come near me. I mean, some do, but they aren't the type I want."

Josh nodded like that made perfect sense. "You're intimidating."

Huh? "Intimidating? Me?"

"Yeah, but if they can't see you, it'll be fine. And then once you've gotten to know each other and you meet in person, Mr. Dream Guy will be in for a lucky surprise."

"But hiding what I look like, isn't that kind of the same as just being me, but wearing baggy old clothes? And what do I do if he asks for a picture?"

Josh thought for a moment. "We'll send him one. From the neck up. I've seen what you girls can do with makeup. All we need to do is make you less attractive, and we can do some photo editing for the finishing touches."

I could do a lot with contouring, and Chloe had mad skills. She'd enjoy the challenge of making me look as awful as possible. It felt wrong though. Mom always taught me how important it was to appear presentable.

"So we make me look really ugly? What if it sends him running?"

"If he runs away after getting to know you, then he's not worth your time. Besides, I'm not sure it's possible for you to look ugly. Let's just bring things down to average."

My heart somersaulted. Even though it was indirect, that was definitely a compliment.

"You think I'm above average?" I grinned up at him.

Josh glanced at my boring taupe—sorry Mom, I mean Tranquil Pebbles—wall before meeting my eyes again. "You're very pretty, Allie. Haven't we already established that? The whole reason I'm trying to help is because guys find you too attractive."

My hopeful grin remained. "Saying guys find me attractive isn't the same as saying you do."

Josh blew out a slow breath. "I *am* a guy, Allie. Haven't you noticed?" He raised his thick eyebrows slightly.

Oh yes, I'd noticed.

And this was so promising. The thought that Josh found me attractive, maybe even *too attractive*, filled me with so much excitement I had to bite my tongue to contain it.

Josh cleared his throat. "What do you think then? Are we going to give the plan a try?"

"I guess so. It's not like there's anything to lose. So I go into the chat rooms, try to forge a connection with someone, and then if they want to see what I look like, we send a picture where I look awful?"

"You don't have to look awful. It's more about masking your potential."

I nodded. "We could get some tips from Noah on that."

"From Noah? What do you mean?"

"Didn't you notice how cute he is?"

Josh gave me a blank look.

"If we got him new glasses and fixed his hair, I think it would completely transform him. He'd be a total hottie." I smiled to myself. Noah had so much potential, it'd be fun to unleash it. I could already imagine how the girls at school would react.

Josh continued staring at me for a drawn-out moment, but

then he smiled as if struck by inspiration. "So you think he's cute? Do you think he might make a good boyfriend?"

Noah? As my boyfriend?

"How well do you know him?" Josh asked.

"I don't really know him at all. We spoke for the first time yesterday."

"What did you talk about?"

"I asked him about his hobbies. But he seemed a little on edge, like he wasn't comfortable around me." I shrugged.

"That's perfect."

"It is?" My boyfriend criteria wasn't all that strict, but I didn't want one who was uncomfortable in my presence.

"Yeah. He could barely look at you downstairs earlier."

Poor Noah had seemed so nervous.

"That's a good thing?" I asked.

"Absolutely. He knows you're out of his league. If he got with you, he'd be the happiest guy on earth. He'd treasure you. Treat you well."

"You think so?"

Josh nodded with enthusiasm, which made me a little sad. He loved the idea of me with Noah, while I loved the idea of me with *him*.

"What were his hobbies?" Josh asked.

"Tutoring." I scrunched up my nose. "That's almost as bad as saying homework."

Josh chuckled. "Tutoring is great. It shows initiative. Wasn't that one of the things you wanted?"

"It shows initiative?"

"Sure. He's using his strengths, in this case knowledge, and turning a profit. That's enterprising. Plus, he's helping people along the way. There's nothing wrong with enjoying that."

I mulled over his words. Maybe he was right. Chloe seemed to enjoy tutoring too, although from the way she described how she'd tutored Nate, they spent most of their time playing video games.

"He also liked tabletop gaming..." I offered, giving an utterly unconvinced shrug.

"Like board games? Ryder played some of the more modern ones with his dad. He said they were a lot of fun." Josh raised his eyebrows and gave me a hopeful smile.

Ryder liked board games? I would never have expected that.

Josh tilted his head, his eyes trained on my face. "What's the verdict then? Do you think it's worth giving Noah a try? Get to know him better and see if you're a good fit?"

I nodded. "I like it more than the chat room idea. But you're forgetting something. What if Noah doesn't want to date me?"

Josh scoffed. "He'd be a fool not to."

Why don't you want to, Josh?

"But I'll ask," he continued. "Then help him out if he needs it. Hopefully give him some confidence and let him know you don't bite."

"I might bite," I teased.

Josh laughed, just like I wanted him to. "In that case, I won't mention it. We don't want to scare him away. What time does the tutoring finish?"

"It's a two-hour session."

Would Josh want to wait? Getting to spend time with him one-on-one like this was rare, and the thought of him staying for so much longer made my heart gallop.

"Do you want me to go?" he asked. "I could come back later, try to catch him before he leaves?"

"No. Stay." I patted the bed next to me.

Josh had been standing by the door for far too long. If he was going to wait for tutoring to finish, it would be crazy to stand for hours. He needed to get comfortable.

That meant on the bed. With me.

11

Josh

"COME ON." Allie furrowed her brow and patted the bed again. "I was only joking about the biting."

I swallowed. I was happy to remain standing over here at a safe distance, but considering I'd have to wait two hours, that would be weird behavior.

I dutifully joined Allie where she wanted me, next to her on the edge of the bed.

She smiled. "It's funny how we don't often get a chance to talk like this. Without Mia."

"Well, you come to the house to see her, not me."

Allie pushed her lips out and bounced her head from side to side as if jokingly questioning whether that was true. "I guess. But I like it when you're there too. It's quiet now you're in college. We miss you."

A twinge of guilt hit my stomach. I'd wanted the full college experience, which meant living on campus, leaving Mia at home alone. She swore blind she didn't mind, and I'd believed her at the time, but now I wasn't so sure.

"How are you enjoying your classes?" Allie asked. "You're studying Advanced Business Management Strategies, right?"

"Yeah." I nodded, impressed she'd remembered my major. "Things are good."

Allie gave me a smile, like she was genuinely happy for me. "What are you learning? How to set up your own business?"

"It's more about business efficiency, but there's a lot about regulations too."

"So, improving someone else's business? You'd go in as a private contractor?"

I loved the intent look of concentration on Allie's face as she questioned me.

"It's not a job, more like a skill set. There are tons of things I could do with it after graduation."

"Do you know what you want to do?"

I paused. Other than Ryder, I hadn't told anyone about my plan. "I'm thinking of setting up my own business. I want to be an electrician."

Allie's eyes widened. "That's so cool. You should totally do it. Follow your dream." She grinned at me. "What sort of things would you, er, electrify?"

I laughed. "I was thinking of going the domestic route. Helping people with home improvements, or fixing things. Making sure everything's safe. It's not the most highly paid option, but I think I'd enjoy it."

Allie nodded with enthusiasm. "We have to let my mom know. I bet she'll have some work for you."

"What does your mom do?"

"Interior design and home staging. But she takes it to the extreme. Complete transformations. That's why she earns so much." Allie shrugged. "I know she's always moving around light fittings and stuff like that."

Interior design. I glanced around Allie's room with a new understanding, and she followed my gaze.

"Yep. Sometimes Mom needs to try out the latest shades of paint."

"You don't mind?"

"Not really. I'm used to it, and occasionally I get an actual color instead of boring neutrals." Allie pulled Mr. Giraffe onto her lap.

"I'm guessing you aren't planning to follow her career choice."

"I don't know what I'll do yet. I don't really have any hobbies, so who knows?" She stared into Mr. Giraffe's shiny black plastic eyes, as if expecting him to have the answer.

"I'm sure you'll figure it out." I put my hand on her arm. Allie's beautiful smile had disappeared, and I wanted it back.

"Thanks, Josh." She looked over to meet my eyes. "Anyway, I'm glad you're enjoying college, but something tells me we'll be seeing you back in Haven Valley more often now?"

"Yeah." I chuckled, moving my hand so I could pet Mr. Giraffe. "I think you're right."

Allie grinned as she watched me shower attention on the plush toy. "I've never seen Mia so happy."

I nodded. "It's weird seeing them together, but if Ryder puts a smile on her face, I'll learn to get used to it."

"It's not just because of Ryder. She's happy about your parents too."

My hand hovered in the air as I stilled. I hadn't expected the conversation to veer in this direction. I hated talking about my parents.

"Mia told me you talked to them for her." Allie smiled. "I don't know what you said, but it made a big difference."

"I'm glad."

I'd sat my parents down and forced them to listen. I'd stayed calm while I gave them a piece of my mind about how their parenting style affected my sister. Yet I'd failed to get out everything I'd intended to say. I didn't tell them how much it affected me too.

"Let's hope it doesn't backfire," Allie said in a teasing tone. "You might have helicopter parents now."

"Not likely." I scoffed. "Mom couldn't even be bothered to tell me Happy New Year."

Crap. I shouldn't have said that out loud.

"I'm so sorry. Mia told me she called—"

"She talked with Mia, and that's what's important." I shrugged.

Allie furrowed her brow. "You don't have to put on a brave face. You're allowed to be upset that your parents are neglectful."

"Neglectful?" I laughed. "It's not like we go hungry. Mia and I have everything that—"

"Emotionally neglectful. Mia tells me everything, Josh, and I remember how you went off the rails. It was a classic cry for attention—" Allie winced, then covered her mouth with her hand. "I'm so sorry. I don't mean to psychoanalyze you. I just feel so bad. You and Mia are like the best people ever, and they just don't seem to…"

Oh hell no, Allie, don't cry.

She moved Mr. Giraffe to the other side of her, then after a quick glance at my well-rehearsed unaffected expression, she leaned over and wrapped her arms around me, taking me by surprise.

Allie gave a lot of hugs, but they were usually quick. This was something else. She held on tight, as if she thought squeezing me hard would make everything better. And if I hadn't been so distracted by the feel of her body pressed against mine, and the deliciously sweet smell of whatever tempting fragrance she'd sprayed herself with, it might have.

I pulled away. This was too awkward. "I'm fine, Allie. I don't want your pity."

"It isn't pity, Josh. It's compassion." She was probably looking at me now, but I stared at the door, unwilling to subject myself to another view of her glossy eyes.

"Either way, it's no big deal," I said. "And you've got it worse. At least my parents are both still—"

If there was an award for being an insensitive oaf, I'd have just won.

"Alive?" Allie finished.

"I'm so sorry, A." I met her eyes. "I wasn't thinking."

"It's okay. I miss my dad, but while he was here, he was the greatest. I'm so grateful I had that." She gave me a heartwarming smile.

Allie's dad passed away from cancer when she was young—I think around seven or eight—right before she moved to Haven Valley and became friends with Mia. I'd never talked with Allie about it, and even though I was sure she'd be open, and she was smiling at me right now, I didn't want to risk upsetting her.

Not thinking about what I was doing, I reached my arm around her and pulled her back into me. She was warm and soft, and she fit perfectly against me.

Allie laughed into my shoulder. "I should bring out all the sob stories if this is how you react."

I wanted to keep her in my arms, but instead I let her go with a slight chuckle and she reluctantly shifted back.

"How did things get so heavy?" I asked. "Let's change the subject?"

"Sure. What do you want to talk about?"

I shrugged, but her earlier comment was finally sinking in, so I narrowed my eyes. "What do you mean, went off the rails?"

I never claimed to be a model citizen, but for an almost completely unsupervised teenager, I thought I did better than okay. Sure, I drank, but that was only a social thing. I didn't smoke, vape, or do drugs, and I always stayed on the right side of the law.

She laughed again. "I just meant with all the girls, and getting into fights."

I couldn't really argue about the girls, but *all* made me sound way worse than I was.

"Getting into fights?"

There had been occasional scuffles, but the only time I'd ended up with bloody knuckles was after some less-than-PG comments about what a couple of so-called friends wanted to do to my sister.

Allie nodded. "Can I tell you a secret?"

"What is it?"

"Last night, I really, really wanted you to punch Chris."

I couldn't stop the laughter from escaping my lips. "You did?"

I'd been so tempted to do exactly that, but I was getting better at resisting my urges. Violence generally didn't lead anywhere good, and I was confident Chris wouldn't go near Allie again.

I gave her a sympathetic smile. "Sorry to disappoint."

"You didn't disappoint." She grinned back at me. "It means a lot to me that you were there last night." She clasped her hands together, pretending to swoon. "You're my hero."

I shook my head. Allie was so damn cute, but the last thing I needed was to be her hero.

That was a job for somebody else, and even though I'd barely even met the guy, I wanted it to be Noah. I had a good feeling about him, but first he needed to agree to a date.

And with the nervous way he reacted to Allie earlier, making that happen might be a lot easier said than done.

12

Josh

ALLIE'S FACE contorted in disgust. "We thought he'd quit after a couple of spoonfuls, but I think Mason wanted to eat the whole tub. He was pulling these foodgasm faces like he was loving it."

I laughed. "A real gastronomic delight."

"Yuck. Not even close. I wouldn't eat ketchup on ice cream if you paid me."

"Does that mean you always choose truth, then? Because you have to do the dares."

She shook her head. "Everybody knows that I—"

"Allie!" Gavin hollered up the stairs. "Where's the money?"

Allie sprang from the bed and rushed to the door. She glanced back at me with a grin. "Let's go get me a date."

I pushed myself up. Somehow, in the time spent with Allie, I'd relaxed and made myself comfortable. I'd been lying on her bed, alternating between looking at her and at the ceiling, while she recounted tales of what I'd missed from the parties Mia never liked me to be home for.

Allie darted out of the room, so I chased after her, coming

to an abrupt stop as I bumped into her at the entrance to the kitchen. She giggled as she looked over her shoulder to give me a smile.

"Where did Mom put the money for Noah?" Gavin asked, closing the drawer he'd been searching through.

"Um, I think it's in the living room," Allie answered, looking at her brother. "Come and help me find it." She led him out of the kitchen, leaving me with Noah, who was zipping up his backpack as slowly as possible.

I stepped over to him. "Hey, man. We didn't get an introduction earlier. I'm Josh."

"Noah." He glanced up before returning his attention to the zipper.

"Do you have a few minutes? There was something I wanted to talk to you about."

Noah brought his anxious eyes up to look at my face.

"Nothing bad. I just wondered what you thought of Allie?" I lifted my eyebrows.

He hesitated for a moment. "I don't really know her, but she seems friendly." He gave me a meek smile, as if unsure whether that was the correct answer.

"Do you think she's pretty?"

A light blush spread over Noah's cheeks. That was a *yes* then, as expected. "Um, yes. Your girlfriend has a very nice smile."

"She's not my girlfriend."

"Oh." Relief washed over Noah's face. "I just assumed…"

"As it so happens, she's single, and she told me she thought you were, and this is a direct quote, *a hottie.*"

"What?" His eyes widened and the redness on his cheeks deepened. "No, she didn't."

"Seriously, she did. I swear I'm not messing with you, and she'll be happy to tell you herself. I just wanted to check what you thought first. Do you want to get to know Allie?"

"Get to know her?" Noah swallowed.

"Yeah. I mean just talking. Something casual to see if you have couple potential."

"Talking?" He looked as if I'd suggested a root canal.

"You don't like talking?"

He winced. "I have a little social anxiety. It's mostly manageable, but talking to girls is…" He shrugged. "Talking to beautiful girls is still a struggle."

"It's still a struggle?" I repeated. "I take it that means you're not seeing anyone?"

He shook his head. "I tried once, but it didn't do much to help. My mom thinks I should go back, talk to a different therapist, but I'm not sure. I read a book on CBT and I think the best thing is just to practice. Put myself out there."

I nodded with encouragement, even though I'd meant my question to ask if he was dating anyone. But I guess the answer to that was obvious. "Putting yourself out there is a great idea. So, you'll give it a shot? Go on a date with Allie?"

"A date? You said casual."

"A casual date. No pressure."

Noah shoved his hand through his hair before staring down at his bulging backpack. "I'm not sure. How will I know what to say to her?"

"I'll help you."

"You will?" He glanced up at me.

"Sure, if you want me to. Besides, Allie can be a chatterbox, so you might not have to say much." I flashed him a hopefully reassuring smile.

"So you'll mentor me?"

Mentoring? That made it sound like hard work, but I'd do what I could if it would help Allie. I nodded.

"And you know how to talk to girls?"

It wasn't something I actively thought about. I just opened my mouth and words came out, but I guess that meant I knew how, and things tended to go well.

I nodded again. "How about we exchange numbers? I'll make sure I'm around before and during your date. Any questions, just shoot them my way."

Noah smiled. He was close to agreeing.

"I know Allie pretty well," I added. "That should make things easier, too."

"How do you know her?"

"She's friends with my sister. You go to Haven Valley High, right? Do you know Mia?"

"I know who she is." He smiled as he paused. "Why are you doing this? Setting me up with Allie."

"Because she deserves it. Allie is the sweetest girl, but she hasn't had much luck finding a boyfriend. I think you two could be perfect together."

"You don't even know me."

"No, but I'm an excellent judge of character. And it's worth a try. Seriously, she'll make an amazing girlfriend."

He hesitated. "But you don't want to date her?"

There was no way I wanted to explain all the reasons for my resistance, so I went with a lie. "I already have a girl, and even if I didn't, getting involved with my sister's best friend wouldn't be the smartest idea."

"You honestly think she likes me?" he asked.

"I know she does."

"And you'll be there to coach me?"

"Yes. I'll be there remotely. It'll be a great opportunity to put yourself out there."

He nodded slowly. "Okay. What's your phone number?"

I smiled. The plan was on.

After exchanging numbers with Noah, I took him through to the living room where Allie was sitting on the couch, pretending to be watching the news on TV.

She switched it off and jumped to her feet. "Hey, Noah. I have your money for tutoring." She handed him some folded bills, which he pocketed with a polite smile.

Then we all stood there.

Allie must have been eavesdropping, but for whatever reason, she was being unusually quiet. I glared at her for a second until she met my eyes and understanding hit.

She beamed her smile at Noah. "This might sound crazy since we don't know each other all that well yet, but I was hoping you might like to go out with me sometime. I think we'd have a lot of fun together. What do you say?"

I couldn't take my eyes off Allie's gorgeous face. It was a relief she was looking at Noah, because I wouldn't have been able to say no to anything she asked right then, and I wasn't sure how any other guy could either. If she continued to struggle with career ideas, hostage negotiator could be a viable option.

Noah nodded. "Yeah, I, er, I'd like that."

"Awesome." Allie smiled again, and it was like she radiated friendliness.

"Great," I said. "Are you both free tonight?"

It wasn't a secret I was playing go-between, so I'd embrace

the role. This way I could speed things up without making Allie look desperate.

"I can't tonight," Noah answered. "It's family night."

"How about tomorrow?" I suggested. I might not be the most attentive coach tomorrow since I'd be busy driving back to college, and that was after helping Mia take down our Christmas decorations. But I didn't want to wait. I'd make it work.

"Tomorrow is my board game club."

"Is that an exclusive club, or can anyone go?"

"Everyone's welcome." He dared a glance at Allie.

"Sounds like fun," she said. Based on her reaction upstairs, I wasn't convinced she was telling the truth, but I figured Noah would be most comfortable on his home turf. And if he was less anxious, things were more likely to go well.

Noah smiled at Allie. "I can pick you up on my way over if you'd like to come along?"

"That would be great. Thanks, Noah."

A few minutes later, with plans in place, I walked Noah to the door, leaving Allie in the living room.

"I'm so not ready for this," Noah said.

"You'll be fine, don't worry."

He nodded. "When I pick her up, should I get out of the car and come to the door?"

"Yes."

"What about the car door? Should I open it for her? It's kind of old-fashioned, and I don't want her to think I'm suggesting girls can't open their own—"

"Open the door. Be as chivalrous as possible. Allie will love it."

He nodded again. "Okay."

"Just try to relax, and seriously, don't sweat the small stuff. She won't judge you."

I reassured Noah a couple more times before he left. Then I returned to Allie in the spotless beige living room.

"I can't believe it!" She pulled me into another one of her hugs before letting go. "The plan is working. And you're going to mentor him?" She grinned.

"So you *were* listening." I shook my head in mock disapproval.

She gave me a bashful smile, then tilted her head as she gazed at me. "Did you mean what you said? That you think I'll make an amazing girlfriend?"

I sucked in a breath. I couldn't imagine a better girlfriend than Allie, but I wasn't about to tell her that. "You'll be okay," I teased. "Noah could do worse. He's lucky to have you."

She swatted at me. "Thanks, but I'm not his girlfriend yet."

No. Not yet. But I would do everything I could to help them build a connection. Because the more I thought about it, the more I hoped Allie would fall for someone like Noah.

Someone safe.

13

Allie

MIA RUMMAGED THROUGH MY CLOSET. "What do people wear to play board games?"

"I have no idea, but we need to pick something baggy." I pointed to the small selection of unflattering clothes that had somehow avoided all my previous wardrobe culls.

"Baggy? Why?" Chloe asked from the doorway. Like Mia, she had brown hair, except hers was cut sharp at an angle below her shoulders. It suited her perfectly.

"So I don't look too sexy for my date."

Chloe laughed.

"Don't laugh," I pleaded. "I don't want Noah to notice my figure."

"I'm sure he's already noticed," she said.

I sighed. "I'm trying to do this right."

Getting to know Noah had been my backup plan, but after overhearing Josh saying he had a girlfriend, my main plan was over, and this was all I had left. This, or the chat rooms.

"And doing it right means you have to hide your figure?" Chloe asked.

"Well, Josh said that guys—"

"Hold up," Mia interrupted. "You're still listening to Josh's advice?"

"Why not? Who else knows more about how guys think than a guy? And he suggested I make myself less attractive."

Mia scrunched her nose in a way that showed she was totally unimpressed. "What is he playing at? You should ignore Josh. He knows nothing about relationships."

"Even though he has a girlfriend now?"

"What? Josh has a girlfriend?" Her mouth dropped open. Hopefully I hadn't blown some big secret. "Since when?"

"I don't know any of the details, and I don't want to know."

Just thinking about it made the jealousy rise up within me, and that was stupid. Josh had always said nothing would ever happen between us, and even though I frequently allowed myself to get my hopes up, this was a reminder that he'd been telling the truth all along.

I needed to focus on tonight. On my date with Noah.

He could be the one.

"Are you sure Josh has a girlfriend?" Mia asked. "That kind of goes against everything he's ever said, and Ryder hasn't mentioned anything."

"That's what I overheard him say, but can we please not talk about Josh? Tonight, I'm all about Noah."

Mia nodded, although she still looked confused.

Getting ready for the big date was a far quicker process than usual. I kept my makeup minimal and chose casual clothes jeans and a loose sweater paired with my favorite winter boots. I didn't need my friends' help, but it was fun just to hang out, even if the conversation did seem to revolve around their boyfriends.

The girls left before Noah arrived, so I waited for him alone. The usual jittery pre-date excitement bounced around inside me, peaking when there was a knock on the door. I skipped over to answer it.

"Hi. You look great tonight," Noah said with enough confidence that I suspected he might have rehearsed it in the car on the way over. It was enough to make me want to hug him.

"Thanks. I'm hoping your board game club is casual dress?"

"Yes. Very casual." He gave me a nervous smile. "Are you ready to leave?"

Noah looked super cute tonight. He still wore the dorky glasses, but his black hair was messy.

"I'm ready."

I followed Noah down to his car, and as we approached, he ran ahead to open the passenger door for me.

"Thank you." I climbed in. Five points for Noah.

Even though the car looked old from the outside, the inside had that new-car smell, and there were tiny models sitting in a plastic tray on top of the dashboard.

"What are those?" I asked.

"The miniatures? They're from one of my games."

"You use them in the game? They aren't ornaments for your car?"

"Yes, I mean no." He took in a breath. "I mean, yes, I need them for the game. But I got a custom paint job, and I enjoy looking at them, so, um, until I play next, I've been leaving them…"

"They look amazing," I said after Noah trailed off. "Can I take a closer look?" I reached out my hand but didn't intend to touch until I got permission.

He nodded, so I took hold of the tray. There was a range of fantasy characters and monsters, all intricately painted.

"Wow, there's incredible attention to detail here."

All I could think of was how Josh would be great at paintwork like this, even though I was trying not to think of Josh. He'd sent me a good luck message earlier, but I hadn't talked to him since he left the house yesterday. Tonight he'd be driving back to the dorms with Ryder, much to Mia's sadness, but he'd promised he would be around if I needed help.

Not that I expected to. Tonight was all about getting to know Noah, so my task was straightforward—encourage Noah to relax. I would do what I could, but Josh was there for him too. And if Josh could somehow put Noah at ease, give him some tips, that was fine by me. I suspected he was already responsible for the improved hairstyle.

I kept the conversation about the models going until we arrived outside a collectibles store. It looked closed.

Noah jumped out of the car and rounded the hood, before opening my door for me again.

"Thanks." Another five points.

Noah had a smile of satisfaction, and I loved that he was trying so hard. He led me toward the building. "The entrance is through the side door."

Inside, Noah took me through to a large room. Lining the walls were shelving units holding store stock, and the floor was set up with tables and chairs, ready for an evening of gaming. There were a few people here already, unpacking board game components onto their tables. One guy stood up and waved us over.

"Ready for the rematch?" he asked Noah. "I've been losing sleep over how to claw back those last two points."

The man, who looked mid-forties, let out a friendly chuckle. He wore a t-shirt that declared *I read the rules so you don't have to,* and he had a rounded figure—lots of him to love.

"You might have to wait for next week," Noah said. "I've brought a friend with me tonight and was planning to start her off easy." He flashed his cute smile in my direction, and the man followed Noah's gaze to me.

"Welcome, friend. It's always good to see fresh faces in here. I'm Big Mick." He stuck his hand out, so I shook it.

"Hi. I'm Allie."

"Good to have you joining us, Allie." He turned his attention back to Noah. "I'm sure she can handle it. She can take Ashley's place."

"Ashley isn't coming tonight?" Noah asked.

"Would you believe that even after two weeks off school, she left all homework until the night before you go back?"

Noah laughed. "Yeah, I'd believe that."

Big Mick looked back at me with his eyebrows raised in hope.

"I don't know what I'm doing, but I'm happy to play whatever," I said.

"You don't have to, Allie." Noah had a smile that told me, despite his words, that he really wanted the rematch. "It's a heavy Euro."

That probably would have meant something to someone else, but all I understood was *this game's going to be complicated.*

"I don't mind, and at least Big Mick can help me out with the rules." I dropped my eyes to his t-shirt.

I was almost definitely about to get swallowed alive by board game sharks, but the contrast in Noah was staggering. As soon as we began talking to Mick, it was like all the tension evaporated from his body. I wanted to keep him here where he was relaxed, even if it meant defeat for me.

"Don't trust his interpretation of the rules," Noah said. "He bends them into whatever helps him the most."

Mick opened his mouth in mock outrage before laughing. "Believe me, I need all the help I can get." He grinned. "Why don't I get everything set up, and you can explain the core concepts?"

I spent the next ten minutes watching Mick prepare the gameboard, while listening to Noah attempt to explain the game. It was all action points this, and victory points that. It was a lot to take in, and while I was happy Noah was in his element, it felt like tonight would be a long, slow slog.

TWO HOURS later and I was loving it. After suffering a crushing defeat at Noah's hands, Big Mick wished us well and left us alone. That was when things changed. Noah introduced me to what he called gateway games, and unlike Mick's confusing choice—which took almost as long to score as to play—these ones were accessible to anyone. Even me.

"That's two reds, two whites, and a green," I proudly announced, returning my chips to the stack and adding the card I bought to my collection.

"Nice job," Noah said, before letting his eyes drop to his phone, which was next to him on the table.

It was on silent, but messages had been flashing up all evening. Somehow, Noah managed to subtly fire off quick replies without seeming rude while I was busy mulling over the best actions to take on my turns.

Even though I couldn't read the messages, I was positive they were from Josh. And whatever advice he was offering was spot on, because Noah was turning into a great date. He was doing everything right.

Noah chose some chips, which represented different gemstones, and then it was my turn again.

"I really like your hair like that," I said. It looked so good, I just wanted to reach out and touch it.

His eyes crinkled at the corners. "You do? Thanks."

"You're welcome. So, you come here every week?"

I hoped he'd invite me back.

"Yes, every Sunday."

"It's fun. Not at all what I was expecting." I glanced around the room, which not too long ago had been full, but was now beginning to empty as the evening drew to a close.

Noah gave me an almost bemused smile. "You weren't expecting it to be fun?"

"Honestly, I wasn't convinced. But I'm glad I'm here. Thanks for giving me a chance."

"Giving you a chance?"

"Yes." I bought another card with my chips. This game was simple enough that we could carry on a conversation at the same time as playing. It was my favorite type. "I guess Josh kind of surprised you with the idea of going on a date with me?"

Noah nodded. "I never in a million years thought that someone like you would want to… with someone like me." He blushed as if embarrassed by his mumbling, and that was when I decided.

Noah might not make my skin tingle from every touch, or make my heart race from a single look the way Josh did. But I liked him a lot.

He was clever, kind, respectful, and fun to be around. Not to mention totally cute. It was all I could ask for in a boyfriend.

Plus, unlike Josh, he seemed to be interested in me, and he was single.

At least he was for now, because I didn't intend to let him stay that way for long. I'd been searching for the perfect boyfriend, and all the signs were pointing to Noah.

I'd finally found him.

14

Josh

"HE SAYS they're on the last game. Should he let her win this one?" Ryder read from my phone.

"Definitely. Allie would love to end on a high note."

He typed out the reply, and the message swooshed away.

"Anything from her?" I asked.

"You don't think I'd tell you?" Ryder glanced over in amusement. He'd had that same expression for the entire car ride so far, ever since I explained how I was trying to help Allie.

I should've asked Ryder to drive, but I hated the thought of other people driving my car, especially when I was there. So instead, I was driving us back to the dorms, and Ryder was tasked with reading my messages and typing out the replies.

"Here's one from Allie," he said. She'd been mostly silent all night, and her last message was to say how well things were going, and that whatever I was telling Noah, to keep it up.

"What does it say?"

"You sure you want to know? I don't think you'll like it."

I scowled. "Just read it."

"She says, about to leave. Is the first date too soon to kiss him goodnight?"

I blew out a short breath. Things were going great for Allie and Noah. This was exactly what I wanted.

"That might be too much for him to handle?" Ryder said, his eyes on me.

"I agree."

"What do you want me to put?"

"Ask Noah. Send a message and ask if he wants to kiss her goodnight."

"Okay." He tapped away on my phone, and the reply came through surprisingly fast. "He says, yes, in theory, but how do I know if she wants to?" Ryder glanced over at me for my response.

I hesitated. "Tell Allie it's too soon."

"You sure, bro? It sounds like they both want to."

I wasn't sure. I wasn't sure at all. The thought of them kissing bothered me way more than it should have.

But then again, I liked Noah. Allie was so much better off with someone like him than with sleazy Chris. I needed to remember the whole point of this.

I sighed. "Tell her she should do it. And tell him that she wants to."

Ryder nodded and carried out my instructions.

There was silence for a minute. They must already be on the way back to Allie's house. Would they see my messages in time? A big part of me hoped they wouldn't. I flexed my fingers around the steering wheel, and I could sense Ryder's eyes on me.

"What?" I gave him a side-glance.

"This isn't only about wanting to protect Allie, is it?" He

was studying me intently, and I hated it. It made me feel I wasn't in control. "Why are you trying to find her a boyfriend? Just make a move."

I considered laughing, playing off his comment as if he was crazy. But I'd been best friends with Ryder for over ten years. He could read me better than anyone.

"Mia might not like it," Ryder continued. "But she can't complain now she's with me. Guess I helped you out there." He let out a light chuckle.

"I'm not going to make a move. Allie's looking for the perfect boyfriend. That's not me."

"Why not? You've been giving Noah instructions all night. It sounds like you know how to be Allie's perfect boyfriend."

"It's just not going to happen. Let's drop it." I made my voice forceful enough that Ryder would know this wasn't something up for debate.

The message got through loud and clear, and he switched to telling me about the catering company that his dad's boyfriend owned. Ryder was hoping to get a part-time job there, and if he was going to continue to cook for me, any experience in the culinary arts was something I'd enthusiastically encourage.

It took about ten minutes before a message pinged through on my phone. If I hadn't been driving, I'd have spent the entire time pacing back and forth until an update arrived.

"It's Allie," Ryder said, opening the message. My heart pounded while I waited for him to read it to me. "She says Noah is an amazing kisser. Lots of exclamation points there. And that they've decided to make things official." He looked over at me with wide eyes. "Wow. Guess that means your job is already done. Impressive. You must be happy?"

Happy? I was trying my hardest to muster that emotion, but it wasn't coming. This was supposed to be exactly what I wanted. Noah would treat her well. Allie could fall in love the way she'd always wanted. They'd be good together.

"You are happy about it, right, Josh?" Ryder lifted his eyebrows, and his lips twisted into a smirk. There had only been a handful of moments throughout my life when I'd wanted to punch my best friend, but this was one of them.

"Shut up." I clenched my jaw and focused my attention on the road ahead.

Ryder waited a few beats before talking again. "Oh, hold up. I read the message wrong. It actually says, I couldn't do it. What if he thinks I'm a toad?"

Relief slammed into me. They hadn't kissed.

The relief was quickly replaced by annoyance. "What the hell, bro?" I shot Ryder a death glare. "You were messing with me?"

"I'm sorry." The apologetic look on his face made me believe him. "But you needed a wake-up call."

"A wake-up call?"

"Yeah. Because this whole situation makes no sense. You obviously like Allie, and she's made no secret of how she feels about you. Weren't you saying you might try having a girl-friend this year? Here's your opportunity. What's holding you back?"

Ryder knew me so well, but he didn't know everything. Not even he knew how broken I was.

Another message arrived, saving me from his questioning.

"It's Noah," Ryder said. "No goodnight kiss, but the date was great. Thank you for all your help. Smiley emoji."

I nodded with fake satisfaction. "I'm not right for Allie, but Noah might be. I don't want to date her."

I was saying it to convince myself as much as Ryder, but as the words escaped my lips, I knew I was lying.

That left me debating the options. Because even though I didn't deserve Allie, I couldn't stop myself from wanting her anyway.

15

Allie

AS I NAVIGATED my way through the hallways of Haven Valley High, it felt as if I'd entered some weird Twilight Zone. There were couples everywhere. Literally everywhere I looked.

I waved as I walked past some of the soccer team guys with their girlfriends. I even exchanged a brief smile with my friend Kai, catching him during the single millisecond he took his eyes away from Emma. I'd tried to get a date with Kai last year, but he'd always turned me down, claiming it was nothing personal, just that he didn't date.

He'd decided it was worth making an exception for Emma, though. Not that I was bitter—they were adorable together— but it was the story of my life.

I shook away my negative thoughts. I was on the cusp of having a boyfriend. Things were looking up, and soon I might be one half of a couple, leaning up against the lockers, stealing kisses in between classes.

I still hadn't seen Noah this morning, although I intended to track him down later. Right now, I had a different target in mind.

Nate.

He was the only one who could help me with my problem. It took a few minutes to find him, and when I did, he—like usual—had his muscular arm wrapped around Chloe.

"Hey, guys," I greeted them.

"Hey." Chloe smiled. "How did it go last night?"

After she'd previously implored me not to share any details, I'd stopped giving Chloe my full after-date recaps. But I now understood that it was only because those dates had been with Nate. She'd been jealous, even if she didn't realize it at the time.

I'd dated him for a few weeks last spring. He'd needed a bit of convincing, but I was thrilled when he eventually agreed to give things a try. It had been my longest relationship so far, and I'd had fun.

Except we'd been missing the fire I was craving. There wasn't even a hint of a spark, and so Nate—feeling the same—had called things off. I'd been disappointed, and when I was still single months later, I'd tried to rekindle things on Halloween, but my attempt failed.

Truth be told, dating Nate was similar to when we were just friends. But with one important distinction. The kissing.

And wow, his kisses were amazing, like he intuitively knew exactly what to do to get a reaction from me. I still got excited thinking about them.

Chloe raised her perfect eyebrows in expectation. Oh, right, she'd asked me a question.

"The date went really well. He might be the one."

"I never would have paired you two up. Noah's so shy, and you're... less so."

Nate snickered, but he gave me a smile. He was happy for me too.

"Guess opposites attract," Chloe continued. "Do you have a second date lined up?"

"Not yet, but there will be one. There's just a minor problem I need to fix first."

"A problem?" Chloe furrowed her brow. "What's wrong?"

"I'm worried I'm an awful kisser."

Nate let out a burst of laughter, and I focused my eyes on him. What did that reaction mean?

"I'm sure you're not awful, Allie," Chloe said. Then, as if remembering our history, she glanced up at Nate. "Right?"

We were totally putting him on the spot, but I needed to know. He dropped his mouth open, then hesitated. My hopes tumbled away. It should have been an easy answer.

"Please tell me the truth, Nate," I said. "I need to know. Am I a bad kisser?"

I debated telling them what Chris said about me kissing like a toad, but I was too afraid of agreement.

"Nate?" Chloe said. "Just answer her."

"No." Nate shook his head of wavy blond hair. "Of course you're not a bad kisser."

That was utterly unconvincing.

I dropped my head into my hands. "I knew it. I don't know why I didn't see it sooner. Everything makes so much sense."

How could I try to kiss Noah now? It would ruin everything.

Chloe elbowed Nate, and he spoke up again "You're not a bad kisser, Allie. I mean it. If Chloe wasn't here, I'd be raving about how incredible you are."

Chloe gave Nate a good-natured scowl, and I could tell she wanted to laugh. But I still wasn't convinced by his praise.

"Rate me," I said. "On a scale of one to ten, where one is like kissing a toad and ten is how you feel with Chloe."

That got me a smile from Chloe.

"I don't know." Nate shrugged. "This feels like a set-up. Like you're both trying to trick me."

"It's not a trick," I said. "Can't you just give me some constructive criticism?" I pleaded with my eyes. I needed to learn to kiss, and Nate could help me.

"Constructive criticism? Fine. You're almost perfect." He glanced at Chloe, and she smiled as if they were sharing a private joke. "But you're a tad full-on. Some guys might find your enthusiasm a little aggressive."

I nodded, fighting the instinct to offer up a defense. Instead, I thanked Nate for the feedback, said goodbye, then stepped away so I could think alone.

Nate thought I was too enthusiastic? It felt like a strange criticism, but at least it was something I could work on.

But it wasn't something I could work on alone.

16

Allie

BY THE END of the school day, I'd convinced myself that kissing lessons would be the solution to all my problems. I'd be able to go into my new relationship with confidence. More than I'd ever had before.

I returned home to the sound of obnoxious male laughter coming from the kitchen. If I hadn't felt so thirsty, I would've slipped upstairs unnoticed and got right back to figuring out a plan.

Mia had tried to argue that Noah probably wouldn't have much experience to compare me against, but that wasn't the point. I wanted to wow him. And most importantly, I wanted to put my doubts to rest, lock them up, toss away the key, and then bury them for good. I did *not* kiss like a toad.

I reluctantly entered the kitchen, and the eyes of five teenage boys all turned to me, landing on different parts of my body.

Gavin was leaning up against the refrigerator. His best friend, Matt, was sitting on the counter—Mom would hate that—along with another greasy-haired boy, Cody? Two more were sitting at the table. I think their names were...

Oh, who was I kidding? I couldn't remember the names of my brother's bad-influence friends. And it wasn't like it even mattered. With any luck, Gavin would come to his senses, and they wouldn't be in his life for much longer.

"Holy guacamole. Are those things real? Come here, babe. Let me check." That was from one of the guys at the table, and he ended with a snicker.

I'd learned years ago that men made crude comments to get a reaction, or just to show off in front of their tribe. The best way to deal was to grit my teeth, hold my head up high, and pretend I didn't even notice.

"Shut up, dude. That's Gav's sister," Matt said.

Gavin shrugged, unconcerned. "I'll let it slide." *Thanks, Gavin. Nice of you to jump to my defense.* "But be careful. Her new boyfriend might beat you to a pulp."

Was he joking? The idea of Noah fighting anyone was impossible to imagine. And that was a little sad. I loved the idea of a boyfriend willing and able to defend my honor.

"You should sic him on Ian," the second guy at the table said, glancing at me. "It might teach him a lesson." He looked at the jerk, Ian. "Objectifying women is not cool, bro."

Ian rolled his eyes. "Shut up, Ethan. Don't pretend you don't want a piece of her."

Ian and Cody laughed, or more accurately, they giggled.

Ethan looked uncomfortable, but remembering why I was here, I stepped over to Gavin and glared at him. "Out of my way. I want a drink."

He shuffled over, but I didn't miss the guilty look in his

eye. It was almost apologetic. Why was he hanging around with these idiots?

I grabbed a cola, then went upstairs, shutting myself away. The peace and quiet would allow me to think through my options for finding a kissing teacher.

If Nate had been single, I would have begged him, but with Chloe on the scene, there was no way that was going to happen. Even if by some miracle she was okay with it, kissing someone already in a relationship was wrong. Even for educational purposes.

That also ruled out the only other guy who I knew in my gut would be incredible. Just imagining Josh's lips on mine got me feeling all hot and bothered.

But he was out of the equation, thanks to some mystery girlfriend. Not that he'd ever have agreed, anyway.

There had to be someone else. I'd kissed more than a few guys while playing truth or dare at parties, but no one stood out as exceptional. I searched my brain for other options, but it was empty.

Just as things were getting so desperate that I was considering going back downstairs and throwing myself at Ethan— he seemed the best of the bunch—my phone buzzed, saving me from my madness.

My lips curved up when I saw who it was.

JOSH

How was the first day back at school? Did you talk to Noah?

I'd half thought that after last night went so well, that Josh might have considered his job over, but he was still invested.

I began to type out my response, but then deleted it. I wanted to hear his voice.

"Hey, A," Josh answered with a light chuckle seconds after I hit the call button.

He was the only one to abbreviate my name, which was already shortened from Alison, down to just one syllable. I liked it a lot.

"Hi. You're checking up on me?"

"Someone has to. You're a loose cannon."

I laughed. "You think I'll get into trouble?"

"Yeah, I guarantee it. It's best not to leave you unsupervised for long." There was teasing in his voice. "But I guess that's for Noah to worry about now?"

"You can still worry about me if you want."

"I can't waste all my time imagining what mischief you might be up to."

"You think it would be a waste of time?" I threw some sadness into my tone.

"If I'm not there to stop you, or to join in, then yeah."

My breath caught. Was I imagining the flirtation in his voice? He was smiling, for sure.

"Do you want to get into trouble with me, Josh?"

There was a pause before he answered. "I want to keep you out of trouble." He cleared his throat, and just like that, the playful mood disappeared and he was back to business. "So, what's the latest on the boyfriend front? Did you see Noah today?"

"Yes. We talked for a few minutes at school. But it was like he was nervous again."

"Give him time. He'll get used to you. Did you set up a second date?"

"No. We talked about going back to the board game club, but it wasn't really a plan, and I think it might be too soon."

"Too soon?" He sounded surprised. "It's nearly a week away. Are you having second thoughts about Noah?"

"Not about Noah." I sighed. "It's the kissing thing. I want to kiss Noah at the end of our next date, but I don't want to do that until I've learned how to do it well."

There was silence on the other end of the line.

"Josh?"

"Is this about the toad thing? Because I already told you. Chris is a jerk. He only said that to hurt you. Why don't you arrange a date with Noah this weekend? I'll be home again, and I'll do what I can to help. If you're still worried about the kissing, then don't do it yet. There's no rush. But don't lose momentum. Keep getting to know each other. And talk to him at school if you can."

"You're coming home this weekend?"

"Ryder wants to, so it's either come with him or be without my car."

Other people might have told Ryder to find his own transportation, but it didn't sound like Josh had even considered that option.

"What about your girlfriend? Won't you miss her?"

"My girlfriend?"

"I'm guessing she's at college, not in Haven Valley, since she didn't come to the New Year's party?"

"What are you talking about? I don't have a girlfriend."

"You don't?" A resurgence of hope swept under me, lifting me into the clouds. Had I somehow misunderstood? "But didn't you tell Noah you had a girlfriend?"

He laughed. "That was a little white lie. To explain why you and I aren't together."

I pondered his words. "Why'd you have to lie to explain it? What's the real reason?"

Why wouldn't he give me a chance?

I squeezed my eyes shut while I waited for his answer. I shouldn't be thinking like this. I should be excited about Noah. But I couldn't help it. Would I ever get over my crush on Josh?

He exhaled. "I've told you before. It wouldn't work between us. You're better off with someone like Noah."

The first part of that was true. He had told me before. Except right now he sounded unsure. His voice was devoid of its usual conviction.

"Anyway, I should go," he said. "But I'll see you this weekend?"

"Yes." I couldn't wait.

"And you'll set up a date with Noah?"

"Yes. I'll ask him."

Although I was no longer sure that was a good idea.

"Great. I'll catch you later. Bye." He ended the call.

That was abrupt, and the fact that he couldn't wait to leave the conversation only fueled my optimism.

Josh was always telling me *no*, but now it felt like his resolve was wavering. I still wanted kissing lessons, and even though I might need to apply a little pressure, I knew who I wanted to teach me.

17

Josh

"MIND IF I ORDER?" Justin asked. "I'm four drinks away from a free mug, but it's your turn to pay." He shot Ryder a hopeful smile.

We were at Caffeine Craze, the on-campus coffee shop, catching up with a friend.

"Does he need another mug?" Ryder asked with a grin, before leaving to follow Justin to the counter.

I chuckled to myself as I grabbed a table next to the window. Justin must have had at least ten mugs by now. It wasn't even like he was a coffee addict; he was way more addicted to collecting loyalty stamps.

We'd been back at college for a few days, and even though classes hadn't started yet, it was almost refreshing the way life had returned to normal. It was beyond me how I'd gotten myself so swept up in my little sister's best friend's love life. But now, I was barely thinking about Allie anymore—at least I was trying not to.

I played my favorite block matching game on my phone for a few minutes until the guys joined me at the table. Justin handed me my usual double caramel cookie crumble iced blend—my savior after many late nights. It had just the right amount of sugar, which by most people's standards was too much. But I disagreed. The sweetest things were the best.

"Did you get all caught up?" Justin asked Ryder.

Some family drama late last year had messed with Ryder's head, and as a result, he fell behind with studying.

"Almost. I would have, but then another distraction popped up." A smile crept over his lips.

"Of the female variety?" Justin asked.

"Yeah. Josh's sister."

"Your sister?" He gaped at me, then looked back at Ryder. "I never pictured you as a risk taker."

Ryder laughed. "It wasn't intentional, but miraculously I live to tell the tale."

Justin's eyes were wide. "Tell me she doesn't look like Josh."

"Thankfully, no." He cringed, before glancing at me with a smirk. "Not that you aren't beautiful, bro."

"Thanks." I rolled my eyes. It was good to have Ryder joking again, and Mia was a core contributor to his great mood.

"Let's see her then," Justin said, so Ryder pulled out his phone and tapped away.

He handed the phone to Justin. "This is from her birthday party. The one in the purple dress."

"Yeah, I can see how she'd be distracting." With a grin, Justin flicked his eyes to me before returning his attention to the photo. I couldn't see what he was looking at, but Mia's dress had been uncomfortably revealing with a split right down the front. "How old is she?"

"Eighteen," Ryder answered.

"So she's legal." Justin looked up at me again, this time with a teasing glint in his eye. I wasn't going to fall for it, so, appearing unaffected, I sipped my drink. Delicious.

"Who's the blonde?" he asked.

My heart thumped. There had been plenty of blondes at the party, but from the awe in his voice, I knew he was asking about Allie.

"That's her best friend," Ryder said. "She's also unavailable though, so put your tongue away."

Unavailable? Was he saying that because of Noah? Or because of me?

Justin made a show of shutting his mouth. "Well, congrats. You're a brave man." He handed Ryder back his phone.

"Thanks." Ryder smiled. "It helped that Josh was distracted too. He didn't even do the hot dog thing yet."

"The hot dog thing?" Justin asked with amusement, switching his attention to me. "What are you planning to do with hot dogs?"

I laughed, then did my best to explain the high-voltage experiment. We stayed in Caffeine Craze for the rest of the afternoon, just chatting and relaxing as more friends joined us and we shared stories from winter break.

Yeah, it was good to be back.

"TONIGHT?" I leaned against my pillow. "But we've only been here five minutes."

Actually three days, but it didn't feel like long.

"I know, but I don't have any plans tonight, so I figured I could sleep over at the house then head back after breakfast," Ryder said. He was already packing clothes into a bag.

"Sleep over?" I didn't intend to raise my voice, but it happened anyway.

He looked up to meet my eyes. "Relax. You know I'm not going to pressure her."

I frowned. Even though I believed him, the thought of Ryder *sleeping over* with Mia put me on edge.

"If you're worried, you could always come back with me. I'm sure Allie would be happy to see you."

"No Allie jokes." I groaned and let my head drop against the headboard. Sometimes I hated that Ryder could read me so well. My usual tactic of deny, deny, deny, wouldn't work on him. He knew I liked her more than I should. "Please, bro. I can't take it."

Ryder laughed. "I'd be more sympathetic if I understood why you were resisting."

Resisting was the right word.

I blew out a long breath. Fine. I'd try to explain.

"Allie's on a quest for true love, and she deserves a guy who can give her that."

"You don't think you can?"

I shook my head. "You know what I'm like with girls. It's only ever been physical."

"I thought that was the old you?"

He had me there, but just because I was finished with hook-ups, it didn't mean I was capable of a relationship.

"She deserves better," I said.

"What?" Ryder gawked at me. He looked genuinely shocked. "Is Allie upset about the other girls?"

99

She'd said something about *all* the girls. There was no pretense. Allie knew what I was like, even though she'd tried to justify my behavior as some kind of cry for attention.

But it hadn't been like that. If anything, I'd just wanted to feel. To work off my frustrations and share a connection. Even if it was only temporary. Because in those moments, it was easy to believe I was the center of someone's universe.

Man, I was messed up.

"You're too hard on yourself," Ryder said, staring at me, as if he could read my mind. "You could have a relationship if you wanted one. From what I've seen, Allie worships the ground you walk on."

I shook my head again. "I can't be the guy she wants."

Ryder frowned, but I didn't want to talk about this anymore. I needed to get rid of him.

So I plastered a fake smile on my face. "Shouldn't you get going? Mia gets grumpy when she's left waiting." I tossed my car keys at him and he caught them.

"You're rushing me off to spend the night with your sister? Guess that shows how much you don't want to talk about Allie." He gave me an almost sympathetic smile. "I'll leave you alone. But for what it's worth, I think you should give her a chance."

I nodded so he'd leave. Ryder slung his bag over his shoulder, then moved to open our dorm room door.

"Ry?"

He glanced back at me.

"Be careful with her."

Ryder laughed. "I'm not sure if you're talking about your car or your sister. But I promise to be careful with them both."

"Thanks."

Going with Ryder was tempting, and it was easy to imagine Allie's reaction if I showed up unannounced. She'd fling her arms around me, her eyes bright with excitement as she squeezed her body against mine.

And that was why I needed to keep my distance. I hadn't heard anything from either of them, but I was hoping Allie had followed my request and set up a second date with Noah. And this time, despite her bizarre insecurities, I was confident things would go even better and end in a kiss.

Noah shouldn't need too much more guidance, but I'd do what I could to kick-start their relationship. Then Allie would have the boyfriend she always wanted.

I'd watch from the sidelines, and that would have to be enough.

18

Allie

A KNOCK on my bedroom door tore me from my fantasies. They'd been getting wilder with each iteration, but since Josh hadn't even agreed to anything yet, it was probably a sensible idea to keep my imagination in check.

Mom had already gone out for what she called a business dinner—anyone else would call it a date. That meant the knocker had to be Gavin.

"Yeah?" I sat up on my bed with intrigue. He almost never knocked on my door.

The door opened, and he took a step forward. He stood fiddling with his fingers by his sides. Was he nervous about something?

"What is it?" I asked.

"Mom's out tonight, so my friends are coming over."

I twisted my face to show Gavin what I thought of that. "Can't you find an empty park or somewhere to terrorize?"

"No. Word's already out and they want to come here." He paused. "I'm just telling you because I thought *you* might want to go out instead."

I laughed. "Seriously? It's not like I'll be anywhere near you. I have better things to do than try to supervise a pack of feral wolves."

Gavin frowned. "I didn't think you'd want to supervise us. I just thought…"

I stared at him. "What?"

He averted his gaze. "Look, I'm sorry about Ian the other day." His eyes drifted back to mine.

"You are?"

I hadn't expected an apology. Maybe there was still some semblance of my sweet little brother left inside this annoying, lanky teenager.

"You should have stood up for me," I said.

"I know."

"That's it? You know?"

He'd been hearing disgusting male comments directed at Mom for all his life, and for the past few years, they'd been flung at me, too. He rarely reacted, but I knew he hated it. Gavin stared sheepishly down at his feet.

"Why are you even friends with those jerks? Aren't you always saying you're the man of the house? You're supposed to want to protect me." I clenched my teeth together. I wasn't someone who often got annoyed, but Gavin's passivity was irritating.

He glanced up with a scowl. "I do want to protect you. That's why I'm suggesting you go out tonight. Besides, it's Josh's job to protect you now."

My heart flipped as I thought of Josh, remembering the way he'd yanked Chris away from my body, the anger burning in his eyes. Josh was an incredible protector. But he'd been doing it voluntarily. It was far from an obligation.

"When did that happen, anyway?" Gavin asked. "I bet Mia freaked."

Wait. Did he think there was something going on between me and Josh? Something outside of my head?

"I'm not dating Josh."

"You're not? I figured from the way you dragged him up here the other day—"

"Nope. We're just friends." I paused. Hopefully that was about to change. "Are you going to answer my question? Why do you hang around with such creeps?"

Gavin shrugged. "They aren't that bad."

I showed him my unimpressed face.

He laughed. "Seriously, they're mostly talk, and Matt's with them all the time, so…" He shrugged again. "But I still think it's better if you go out."

"Fine. I'll think about it."

"Thanks." He gave me a relieved smile before slipping out of my room and shutting the door behind him.

I didn't like the idea of running away from Gavin's friends, but equally, I'd prefer to avoid an encounter, so I picked up my phone and called Mia.

"Hey. Can I come over tonight? Gavin's creepy little friends are about to invade my house."

"Tonight?" Mia hesitated. "I guess if there's nowhere else to go, but I just talked to Ryder. He's on his way here."

"With Josh?" My heart leaped. Maybe I'd get those kissing lessons sooner than expected.

"No, it's Ryder on his own. I'm sorry, I don't have time to talk right now. I want to take a shower before he arrives. Are you going to come over?"

"Of course not. I'd never get in your way. But I want a full report after Ryder leaves."

"I know you do, but that won't be until the morning."

"What? He's staying the night?"

Mia laughed. "I've got to go. Talk tomorrow."

Then she hung up, leaving me with so many questions.

THE NEXT DAY AT SCHOOL, I hunted Mia down to get answers.

"Mia, I need to know everything!" I took hold of her arm and maneuvered her into the bathroom, where we could talk in private. "Why are you leaving me in suspense?"

A huge grin spread across her face.

"You're glowing," I said, and it was more of an accusation than an observation.

"I'm just happy. But to put you out of your misery, nothing happened."

"Are you serious?" I couldn't hide my disappointment. Even though I'd been envious, I'd been so excited for her.

"Not what you're thinking, anyway."

I bit my lip in confusion. Mia was crazy about Ryder, and all signs pointed to him feeling the same. Didn't they want their relationship to progress? "Why not?"

"We've only just gotten together. I don't want to rush into something physical, and Ryder respects that." She hesitated, and her lips twitched up. "He slept in my room though."

"In your bed?"

She nodded.

"With you?"

"Yes," she answered through a laugh. "But I want this to go well, so we're going to take it slow."

I nodded. That was their choice to make, but if I was sleeping in the same bed as the guy I was in love with, I'd jump at the chance to take our relationship to the next level.

"It was amazing though," Mia continued. "I loved having him there."

"I'm so happy for you."

"Thanks. I'm sorry about leaving you stranded. Did you find somewhere to escape Gavin's friends?"

"I stayed at home in the end. No biggie."

After scrolling through my contact list, I'd been unable to find someone to impose upon.

I would've asked Chloe, but she'd just moved into a new apartment with her family. I figured she wanted to get unpacked and settled in before having friends over, since she hadn't invited us yet.

I even considered calling Noah to see if he wanted to meet, but after barely any contact following our date, I wasn't sure of our relationship status. I'd had fun at the board game club, but did we have any chemistry? Noah hadn't attempted to seek me out, so it was hard to determine if he was even interested.

And although I was supposed to be setting up a second date, ever since finding out Josh was still single, he'd infiltrated all my waking—and sleeping—thoughts.

It wasn't fair to pursue Noah. Not while my heart refused to give up hope for someone else.

Josh would be home tomorrow for the weekend, and I'd be waiting.

I knew exactly what I wanted, and this time I intended to get it.

I wouldn't hold back.

19

Allie

I FIDGETED on Mia's couch, the excitement building in my bones. Everything was planned out in my head. I'd win Josh over this time. I just knew it.

"I really don't think it's a good idea," Mia said.

"I know you don't, but you'll still support us, right? Just like Josh supports you and Ryder?"

Mia frowned. "Support you in a relationship?"

"That's the end goal."

Mia knew my intentions, but she was worried that if I actually managed to seduce Josh, it would only be a onetime thing, and that I'd end up with a broken heart. I was going to prove her wrong.

Mia sighed. "What about Noah?"

"I already talked to Noah this morning. I explained that I just wanted to be friends, and he was cool with it. And we *are* going to be friends. I'm even going to play board games with him again."

"But what if Josh turns you down? You won't want to try things with Noah?"

"I don't know. But either way, I think it would be good for Noah to get to know me better as a friend. Just so he's more relaxed, and then if things change in the future…" I shrugged. "But I can't think about that right now. I know what I want, and I'm one hundred percent focused on getting it."

Mia cringed a little. "Just promise me you won't expect too much. And if Josh says *no*, respect that."

"Don't worry, I won't force myself on him."

Not that I hadn't considered it. Taking him by surprise and planting my lips onto his. I was one hundred and one percent sure he'd kiss me back.

"You should be encouraging me," I said. "Because if I'm keeping Josh busy, he won't be paying any attention to you and Ryder."

Mia laughed. "Well, in that case, good luck."

It was another twenty minutes before Josh and Ryder arrived. I jumped up from the couch at the sound of the front door opening. Mia followed my lead, and we went over to welcome them.

"You made good time," Mia said as Ryder pulled her into a hug, sneaking a quick kiss as he did it.

"Yeah." Ryder smiled at her. "I told him to put his foot down."

Watching Mia and Ryder together made my heart ache. They were so cute, and it was sweet how Ryder wanted to rush back to see her again. I wanted what they had so much.

"We should give you some privacy," I said, linking my arm through Josh's. He glanced down at our arms, as though the contact confused him. "Let's go upstairs, Josh. I need to talk to you."

I nudged my head toward the staircase, and Josh let me

guide him upstairs, and all the way down the hallway to his bedroom.

We went inside, and I pushed the door closed behind us.

I didn't want to end our physical contact, but I was confident Josh wouldn't allow me to cling on to his arm forever, so I released him.

He smiled. How was it possible for a mere mortal to be so attractive? Josh moved to sit on his bed, but then stood up again, and instead leaned against the wall.

Apparently settled, he looked at me. "Are you ready for the big second date?"

I shook my head. "We haven't set up a second date."

Josh furrowed his brow. "I thought you were going to. What happened?"

"It's the kissing. I can't go on any more dates until I learn how to kiss."

He opened his mouth, and he was probably going to tell me I was being stupid, but I didn't give him a chance.

"I went to ask Nate, because he's an incredible kisser, and I was hoping he'd be able to give me some kind of critique. Tips to improve."

Josh's mouth was still open, a slight look of disbelief on his face.

"He told me I was too enthusiastic," I continued. "But that was all. I need more specifics so I can improve. I need someone who I can trust to be honest with me."

I slinked over to where Josh was standing, then I bit my lip and gazed up at him with big, hopeful eyes.

He shook his head. "I know what you're thinking, A, but I can't."

"Please, Josh? It doesn't have to mean anything."

He let out his breath, and I reached up to put my hand on his shoulder.

"If you don't want to do it, maybe you could ask one of your college friends for me? Someone with lots of experience. And then you'd stay to watch, right? To make sure he doesn't take advantage?"

Josh frowned. He liked that idea about as much as I expected him to. "Allie..."

I raised my eyebrows, then placed my free hand on his other shoulder. "It's just a kiss. Help me out?" I stared up into his dark eyes. I never normally got this close to Josh, but it wasn't enough, so I inched my body even closer.

The air was thick, full of tension.

He wanted to kiss me. I could feel it. But for some frustrating unknown reason, he was still resisting.

He needed to give in.

"Please, Josh." I moved my right hand from his shoulder to his neck. Then I tilted my head.

His gaze dropped to my lips. That was the signal I'd been waiting for.

Not wanting to give him a chance to debate with himself further, I pushed forward, softly pressing my lips against his.

My heart hammered. *Don't push me away.* There was a second of hesitation before Josh accepted defeat.

He swept his lips over mine, enticing me to get even closer, then welcoming me as I moved in for more.

My heart was going to explode. I'd been waiting my entire life for this kiss. And it had been worth the wait.

This was everything.

I'd been non-exclusively crushing on Josh for as long as I could remember, but now it was only him. I didn't want any other guy. It was all Josh. All the time. I was a complete goner.

How could I even begin to describe this feeling?

It was tingly and electrifying, but above all, it was right.

Josh stroked his fingers over my neck while our tongues danced. I'd expected him to grab at my body, and I wanted him to, but he was touching me so hesitantly, so softly, his hands tracing over my skin.

It was tender, and my heart swelled from how much I trusted him. He'd never told me how he felt about me, but right now, he was showing me, and there was no doubt in my mind.

He wanted this too.

20

Josh

I PULLED AWAY FOR AIR. I couldn't handle this. I'd kissed my fair share of girls before, but it had never been like this. Never with someone I cared so strongly about.

Allie stared into my eyes, unblinking. "Wow, Josh."

The breathy way she said my name turned me on even more, and I couldn't stop myself from dipping my head until we were connected once again.

This was such a stupid thing to do, but as of yet, I had no regrets.

Allie smiled against my lips. She was the sweetest thing to enter my life, but we had to stop. The more I kissed her, the more I wanted.

I'd already taken too much, so I gathered every morsel of willpower, and then, since I was between her and the wall, I gently pushed her away.

She swallowed. "Well?"

I took a couple of steps to the side. I needed distance to wake me from her spell. "You were fine."

"Fine?" Her expression dropped. "That's only a tiny bit better than barely acceptable."

A smile tugged at my lips; she was too adorable. She wanted me to be honest, but there was no way I could tell her what I thought. That our shared moment had been the best kiss of my life. That all I wanted to do right now was step back into her and do it all over again.

Again and again.

I couldn't explain how for a moment it gave me hope, made me forget I was broken. That I'd felt maybe I actually could have a relationship, and that what I had to offer might be enough.

But I was back on earth now. My head was out of the clouds. So, instead of stepping closer to her the way my body wanted to, I leaned farther away. "You want a better word than *fine*? How about..." Incredible. Mind-blowing. Sensual. "Great."

"Great?" She stared up at me with a look of despondency. "I'm still not sure..."

"Really great."

Allie gave me a small smile, then scratched at her cheek. "Not toady?"

I laughed. "Not at all toady. Honestly, A, I swear you have nothing to worry about."

"Do you really mean that?" Her eyes raked over my face, as if trying to read the true meaning of my words. "What would you give me out of ten?"

Out of ten? That kiss went to eleven. But again, I couldn't let her know how much it had affected me.

"A solid eight point five. No, scrap that. A nine."

Her smile returned, and then an almost predatory gleam

appeared in her eyes. "So what you're saying is that there's room for improvement. Will you help me?"

My retreat had done nothing to save me, and Allie closed the distance between us in a single stride, stopping when her body was mere inches away from mine.

She placed her hand on my chest, then gazed up at me with her huge brown eyes. "You were incredible, Josh. I want to be a ten too. Teach me how to kiss like that?"

I swallowed hard, a surge of pride rushing through my veins. She thought I was a ten?

But was she asking for kissing lessons? There was no way I could agree to that. Could I? Not when I was already teetering on the edge. I was trying so hard to resist, and if tonight taught me anything, it was that I was going to have to try a lot harder.

Allie was crowding me, and I couldn't think, so I shifted over to perch against my desk. "You don't need kissing lessons." I laughed it off.

She sighed, then followed me to my desk, standing in front of me again. "How will I ever get better? I need guidance. I need practice."

"You can practice with Noah." I hated the idea as soon as I said it.

"Maybe." She hooked her arms around my neck. "But I'd rather practice with you."

She was so close. Too close.

"Allie." I shook my head, then reached my hands up to rest on her arms, ready to remove them. But she didn't wait around, and instead Allie tilted her face toward me while gently pulling me closer.

She wasn't being forceful. I could have stopped her. But

after resisting Allie for so long, now that I'd had a taste, I didn't want to resist anymore.

Our lips met again, and the fire was still there.

I pulled her into me, wrapping my arms around her as I took charge.

Allie matched my enthusiasm, the way I knew she would.

I was desperate to touch her, to explore her curves, but that was a line I wasn't willing to cross. So I kept my hands on her back, before raising them to her neck and around to cup her face.

Her skin was soft, smooth, and warm under my fingers.

Why had I been fighting this? Everything I'd been craving was right here.

Allie moaned against my mouth, making my heart pound even faster.

Whatever was happening, she was feeling it too. And even though the logical part of my brain knew I was setting myself up for disaster, I couldn't stop.

This was all consuming.

I ramped up the intensity, giving the kiss everything I had, until Allie pulled away with a gasp.

No! I don't want this to end.

"Tell me what to do," she murmured. And then she was back, teasing my mouth with her tongue.

I had no words of wisdom. No sage advice. How could anyone improve upon perfection?

This was going to ruin me.

A loud rapping on my bedroom door ended our moment. Allie jumped back, out of my grasp, leaving me cold and empty—she belonged in my arms.

She stared at me, almost in surprise, while we both stabilized our breathing. But she'd asked for this. She had to have known...

There was another knock on the door.

"Yeah," I called out.

The door opened to reveal Mia. Her eyes narrowed as she took in the scene. She wasn't stupid. It was obvious she'd interrupted something. "Mom's on the phone. She wants to talk to you." Mia held her phone out, offering it to me.

My already pounding heart somersaulted.

Mom wanted to talk to me? This never happened. Maybe my conversation with her about Mia had prompted some thinking? Maybe she was going to make an effort with me, too? I walked toward Mia and took the phone. Then I glanced back at Allie.

She reacted as if being pulled from a daze, her mouth widening into a grin, and her eyes full of hope and excitement as she looked at me.

"We'll talk later," she said as she moved past me to join Mia at the door.

I nodded, returning her smile.

What would happen next? Was I actually going to attempt a relationship with Allie?

The kisses had changed everything. I couldn't imagine going back to not having that in my life.

Allie grabbed hold of Mia's arm, and they left my room, the door slamming shut behind them.

I took a deep breath, feeling like the luckiest guy on the planet, then I put Mia's phone to my ear.

"Hi, Mom." My voice did nothing to hide my joy. That she wanted to talk to me filled my soul with optimism.

"Hi, baby. Just a quick one. Do you remember if I bought the blue blouse with the butterfly print?"

"What?"

"On our after-Christmas shopping trip. I already asked Mia, but she couldn't remember, so I thought it was worth checking with you before I get her to search my closet. Do you know the one I mean? Blue with yellow butterflies."

"What?" I asked again, louder this time. Mom wanted to ask me about a blouse? I'd tagged along on their shopping trip in an attempt to spend time together, and I'd been tasked with carrying her purchases. But I couldn't remember what she'd bought, and I didn't give a damn.

This was why she wanted to talk to me? No *how are you?* or *what's going on in your life?* She didn't want to know about anything except a stupid blouse.

"Oh shoot. You don't remember, do you? Never mind."

"Mom, is that all—"

"Hold that thought, your father's in my other ear." Her voice went quieter. "Yes, I'll be right there. No, nothing important. It's just Josh."

I gripped tighter onto Mia's phone, the rage and rejection building up inside me. Nothing important? Just Josh?

Maybe it was finally time. Time to give Mom a piece of my mind. I shouldn't still care. It shouldn't matter anymore. I'd been hanging onto the last scrap of our battered relationship for Mia's sake, but now my fury was close to erupting down the phone.

And it would have, but Mom returned to our conversation for only the two seconds required to say *got to go* and to make a kissy noise before hanging up.

It was a slap in the face.

Just minutes ago, I'd been on top of the world. But that feeling was destroyed, and now I remembered who I was.

I needed to get out of here.

21

Allie

"OKAY, ARE YOU READY?"

I'd sat Mia down on her bed. She'd been reluctant to come with me since Ryder was waiting for her downstairs, but the most exhilarating moment of my life so far had just happened. I needed to share the excitement. Ryder could wait a few minutes.

"I'm guessing your plan worked?" Mia didn't look as excited as she should have.

I nodded, barely containing the surge of adrenaline as I flung myself down opposite her on the bed. "It was incredible."

"Incredible, huh?"

"You have no idea." I exhaled a long, slow breath and stared up at the ceiling. "Don't tell Chloe this, but he totally blew Nate out of the water. Best. Kisser. Ever. And the way he used his tongue to—" I shivered, remembering the feel of him against me, even though the memory was already becoming less vivid. We needed to do it again, and soon.

I glanced over at Mia. "Words cannot describe."

She screwed up her nose. "Please don't describe it. But what now? Did Josh think he was helping you with some crazy learning to kiss scheme, or did he actually say he wanted to be your boyfriend?"

"He didn't say anything. You interrupted us." I propped myself up on the bed to shoot Mia a pointed glare before collapsing back down with a giggle. Josh hadn't needed to say anything though. His actions made his feelings abundantly clear.

"Allie, I know you're excited about this, but Josh is Josh. He's never had a girlfriend before, and he's always said he doesn't want one. You need to talk to him before getting your hopes up."

I sighed. Mia could be such a party pooper where her brother was concerned. She did have a slightly valid point though, and I would talk to Josh. As soon as he finished with his mom, we would have a heart-to-heart. Make plans.

And that he was talking with his mom was great news. He wasn't as open about it as Mia, but I could tell how much the lousy parenting affected him too. Mia's relationship with her parents was already improving, and I hoped so much that Josh could have the same.

Mia stood. "Let's go downstairs. Ryder's waiting."

"I want to wait for Josh. I'll go back to his room."

"No. Leave him alone to talk to Mom."

"Of course. I wasn't going to barge in. I'll just loiter outside his door until he comes out."

Mia rolled her eyes, but she laughed, and then hooked her arm over my shoulders as we walked along the hallway to the stairs. Mia headed down, but I continued going, stopping as I reached the door to Josh's room.

I couldn't hear anything from inside, but I wasn't about to put my ear to the door and eavesdrop, so instead I paced. There was still too much adrenaline in my system. I needed to burn it off.

I'd been pacing for a few minutes, and still hadn't calmed down, when Mia and Ryder approached.

"What's wrong?" I asked as I took in the concern on their faces.

"Josh is gone," Mia answered.

Gone?

"What are you talking about? He's talking with your mom." I glanced at the bedroom door. I hadn't heard a peep from inside, but he was in there. Wasn't he?

Mia held up her phone, which I hadn't noticed she was clutching. "I'm so sorry, Allie, but he left."

That didn't make any sense. I knocked on his door, then opened it without waiting for an answer.

It was true. Josh was gone.

"I don't understand…" A wave of panic swept over me. Josh had enjoyed our kisses; I was sure of it. But was I too enthusiastic? Did I scare him off? Or had something bad happened with his mom?

"He was really upset," Ryder said. "He handed me Mia's phone then said he was leaving. He didn't even want to play basketball."

I furrowed my brow in confusion.

"He'd normally calm down by shooting hoops," Ryder explained. "But he said no. He wanted to be left alone."

"What do we do?" I asked. If Josh was upset about me, we could talk it out, and if it was because of his mom, I'd hug him and squeeze him for as long as it took until he felt better. "Should we go out looking for him?"

Mia pulled me into her arms. "We wait. He'll come back when he's ready. He knows we're here for him."

I nodded over her shoulder. Yes, Josh knew that, but it didn't feel like enough. I wished I could actually be there for him.

Mia released me. "Let's go downstairs?"

"I'll wait here," I said. "I don't want to be a third wheel."

Mia tilted her head to the side as she inspected me. "You're not a third wheel. It's not like we're on a date."

Ryder gave me a smile in agreement. They were both super considerate, but I still didn't want to intrude.

I sat down on the low-pile carpet. "Thanks guys, but I'll wait here."

Mia frowned. "If you're sure?"

"Absolutely. He probably won't be long."

Her frown deepened. "He might be. He might not even come home tonight." She shared a look with Ryder. "Are you sure you want to wait here? It might be best to go home…"

I shook my head. I was staying put.

Whatever was going on, Josh was hurting. He'd come back at some point, and when he did, I'd be here for him. And then I'd do whatever I could to make him feel better.

22

Josh

I BLEW out a breath and stared through the windshield at warehouse #3. I'd gotten into my car, not even knowing my destination.

But here I was. It was only a week after I'd been here, tailing Allie. Trying to make sure she didn't get hurt...

My phone had been making noise for the entire drive, so now I was stationary, I checked it. There were the predictable messages of concern from Ryder and Mia, who I also had missed calls from. Allie had left a message too.

ALLIE

I hope you're ok. Please come back

She'd ended the message with three hug emojis, but they were rosy-cheeked and way too happy looking, like they wanted to cuddle me to death.

If I went back, Allie would doubtless have the same expression. She was the sweetest thing, and definitely way too good for me.

You're such an idiot for kissing her.

I'd let things go too far, and now hurting her was inevitable. But I figured it was better to show her who I was now, before letting her get in too deep.

I swallowed down the guilt and fired a quick response back to Mia, telling her I was okay—I hated for her to worry—but that I'd probably be out all night.

Then, not interested in reading her guaranteed response pleading for me to come back and talk, I switched off my phone and left the car.

The inside of the warehouse was exactly the same as before. Even the pounding music sounded identical. The DJ could probably get away with one song on repeat without anyone noticing.

A leggy blonde caught my eye. She pushed her lips together before smiling, then she stuck her head out to the side to listen to the friend saying something in her ear. Blondie grinned, her eyes never leaving my face.

She was a contender, but she wasn't who I was searching for tonight. I wanted to find the sexy girl from last week. Purple Girl.

I shot Blondie a confident smile but continued moving. My eyes scanned over the sea of dancers, focusing on anything the right hue. But Purple Girl might be Pink Girl or Green Girl by now. Something told me she wasn't the type to maintain the same hair color for long.

A man on a mission, finding Purple Girl was all I allowed myself to think about, and I spotted her after a few minutes of wading through the crowds—Blue Girl.

My feet carried me toward her until I was on the periphery of her little group of friends, all waving their arms in time to the bass.

Blue girl twisted to face me, as if tipped off by her friends staring behind her. "Hey there. You came back."

I flashed her my smirky smile. A look I'd perfected, and that girls seemed to love. Go figure. "I wanted to dance with you."

She responded by pressing her body against mine. I didn't care about dancing, but even I wasn't forward enough to tell her what I wanted to do yet.

"I'm Sal," she said.

"Josh."

Take away my troubles, Sal. I want to forget.

We danced for the rest of the song, and the next one, grinding against each other. That had to be enough.

"Want to find somewhere more private?" I asked.

"Sure." Sal smiled up at me. She was taller than Allie, but…

Don't think about Allie.

Sal led me toward the restrooms and down a dimly lit corridor, where the assault on my eardrums lessened.

"I didn't think I'd see you again," she said.

"I couldn't resist," I answered with a smile. I couldn't resist Allie, and as a result I'd made a huge mistake. And even as I gazed down at Sal, something inside of me was screaming out not to make another one.

Sal ran her tongue over her top lip. Then, grabbing fistfuls of my shirt, she pulled me down. Her kiss was hot, passionate, but it left me cold. Empty.

Damn. I'd dreaded that this would happen, but there was no denying reality.

Things weren't the same anymore.

What the hell do I do now?

23

Josh

THE LIGHTS WERE on when I arrived home around 1 a.m., and Allie's car was still parked outside our house.

That she waited for me while I'd been with Sal sent guilt coursing through me, and I was grateful that at least I'd come home alone.

"Josh!" Mia barreled toward me as I stepped through the front door. She wrapped her arms around me for little more than a second before pulling away. "You turned your phone off!" She thumped at my arm. "You know the rules. We don't ever do that."

Those were our parents' rules. They demanded we were always contactable for emergencies, or more accurately, on the off chance that they wanted something while they were traveling the world and leaving us behind.

"Sorry. I just needed some time to myself. You didn't need to wait up."

Mia frowned, concern etched into her forehead. I was such a jerk to run off and leave her worrying. A move I regretted now that my mood had stabilized.

"What happened?" she asked. "You got upset after talking with Mom?"

Bingo, little sis. I hoped with every fiber of my being that Mom's efforts with Mia would continue. I'd thought about it at length, and I was fairly sure that our parents did love her. She'd always been the pretty dancer, so that worked in her favor. Mom had always relished dressing her up and showing her off. I, on the other hand, was nothing to them.

"It doesn't matter. It was a reality check, but I'm fine now. Don't worry." I moved fast, bopping Mia on the nose before she could stop me. I wanted to get back to normal, and playfully annoying Mia was a constant I always got a kick out of.

Mia scowled and swatted the air in front of her face, as if she thought I might repeat the action, and that she'd need to protect herself.

Ryder joined us by the front door. "You okay, bro? Want to go outside?"

I shook my head. "All I want is sleep." I'd already relaxed, so my usual basketball therapy wasn't required tonight. "Allie's still here?"

"She refused to leave," Mia answered. "Even after you said you'd be out all night."

She hesitated, and I could see the conflict in her eyes.

"What is it?"

"She really likes you."

Mia was expecting a bad outcome, but I couldn't deal with a lecture right now, and it wasn't like I didn't already know Allie's intentions. She'd never attempted to hide her feelings, and it made me feel even worse about everything that went down tonight.

"Where is she?"

"Upstairs. She insisted on waiting outside your bedroom."

Allie was absent from the hallway outside my room, and it wasn't until I pushed open the door that I found her.

She was lying on my bed, a gentle rumbling coming from her adorable sleeping form. How could I wake her when she looked like an angel?

I stood in the doorway and stared. People always looked so vulnerable when they were asleep, and Allie was no exception.

She let out a loud snore, and it was a struggle to contain my laugh. I managed to hold it in though, and instead crept through my room and to my bathroom, where I got myself ready for bed while considering how to handle the situation.

I had a plan, but Allie was already tugging on my heart-strings. Did I have the strength to go through with it?

When I stepped back into my bedroom, my bedside lamp was on.

"Josh?" Allie sat up. "Are you okay?"

"Yeah." My voice sounded gruff.

I wanted to tell her she shouldn't have stayed. That she should be at home in her own bed right now. Not here, on top of mine. Because her being here, looking all sleepy and sexy, was dangerous.

"Where did you go?"

I sighed. I wasn't a liar, and Allie deserved the truth. With any luck she'd label me a scumbag and move on to someone worthy.

"I went back to the warehouse on Spring Brook Road."

"You did? Why?"

I sat down next to her on the bed. "I met a girl last week, and I wanted to see her again."

129

Even though she was trying to hide it, the hurt was all over Allie's face. "The one with the purple hair?"

I nodded, surprised Allie had noticed her.

"I'm so sorry," I said. "We never—I never should have kissed you. I hope you didn't get the wrong idea."

It wasn't a question, because I knew full well what ideas she'd been having. I'd totally led her on.

"It's not your fault." She swallowed, and it was as if she was swallowing the truth, because it *was* my fault. I should have fought temptation. "I threw myself at you. You think by now I'd have learned to take no for an answer." Allie let out a dry laugh before continuing. "So, your girl from tonight, is she here? Do you need me to get out of your room?"

I shook my head. "She's not here. And you didn't throw yourself at me. I take responsibility for what happened between us earlier."

"Did our kisses mean anything to you? Anything at all?" She stared into my eyes, and I had to look away to prevent her from reading my face.

"It was only a test." Guess I was a liar, after all. "To make sure you don't have any amphibious qualities."

I glanced back to see Allie's mouth twisting into a tiny, yet sad, smile. She was so beautiful.

"And you passed with flying colors," I said. "So now you're all set for Noah."

She reached out to put her hand on my forearm, her warm fingers wrapping around, holding on. "I don't want Noah. I want you."

Damn. She was going to make things difficult.

"The girl with the purple hair. What happened? Did you…"

"We kissed," I admitted, the guilt lodging in my throat.

Allie's eyebrows lifted, almost as if she was hopeful. "That's all?"

Should I lie? Let her think we'd had sex? Make her hate me so she'd move on? Long term, it would have been a kindness, but the thought of Allie hating me tore me to pieces.

I nodded. "That's all. We talked in my car, but I couldn't go through with anything else."

Couldn't go through with? My words were only making things worse. She needed to believe our kisses didn't matter to me.

Allie bit her lip. "What did you talk about?"

My parents. And you.

Sal had outright asked me about *the girl I'd been watching last week,* and somehow I'd poured my heart out. It was so much easier to talk to a stranger, someone who wouldn't try to argue and tell me I was wrong. Sal had been a great listener.

"Nothing much," I answered.

"But she helped you feel better?"

I met Allie's gaze. I'd expected to see jealousy or maybe even annoyance in her eyes, but instead they were full of concern. That was so Allie, and it made my heart beat even faster for her. I gave a small nod.

She smiled. "I'm glad. Do you want to talk about it with me, too? Whatever your mom said?"

"No." I loved that she cared, but I didn't want to give Mom any more headspace tonight.

"Okay." She paused for a moment, then blew out a loud sigh and squeezed my arm, which she still hadn't released. "I honestly thought we had something. Kissing you was incredible for me, and you can deny it if you want, but I know you enjoyed it too."

"Allie, I…" I had no answer.

"What would it take? For you to give me a chance. That's all I'm asking for."

I couldn't take my eyes off her. She had a hopeful smile, like she'd never give up, no matter the odds. I loved her tenacity, even though she was making it nearly impossible to resist.

"You don't think I'd make a good girlfriend?" She bit her lip and my eyes dropped.

Was she for real? Did Allie think I was holding back because of a failing of hers? That couldn't be further from the truth.

"You would. We've already been over this. You'd be an amazing girlfriend. But I'd make a terrible boyfriend."

"That's a risk I'm willing to take." She leaned over and planted a tender kiss on my lips. Then, when I didn't pull away, she kissed me again.

I reached up to cup her cheek in my hand. I should have been putting an end to her affection, but all I wanted was more.

Man, I was weak.

This wasn't what I'd planned at all. But as I accepted that I was giving in, my mood lifted. It sounded so crazy, but by not stopping her kisses—which were staying gentle, yet somehow increasing my pulse each time she came in for another—was I agreeing to be Allie's boyfriend?

24

Allie

IT TOOK LONGER for Josh to pull away than I expected.

"Allie, stop. We can't do this."

I leaned back in, then softly brushing my lips over his, I murmured, "Yes, we can."

The way Josh responded when I kissed him again confirmed that his objections were baseless. He wanted this. I knew it. I could feel it.

I kissed him harder, wanting to up the intensity. Wanting him to get lost in the moment. To forget whatever doubts he had about me.

He went with it for a few frantic seconds, kissing me with a passion I'd only dreamed of before. But then he pulled away again, his breathing heavy. "Okay, fine."

"Fine?" I grinned. "That still doesn't sound overly enthusiastic to me, but I'll take it." I tried to move in for another kiss, but Josh brought up his hand to block me.

"Wait," he said. "Are you absolutely sure this is what you want?"

Am I sure? Was he kidding?

"I like you so, so much, Josh. I think we'll be incredible together." I took hold of his hand with both of mine and gave him a hopeful smile.

He stared at our hands before gazing back into my eyes. I wanted to kiss him again so badly, but this felt like crunch time. I needed him to agree to date me.

"We need rules," he said.

"Rules?"

He nodded. "You're so damn tempting. If we're going to do this, I want it to be for the right reasons."

I nodded in agreement, even though I didn't have a clue what he was talking about.

"I think you could do a lot better than me," he continued. "But since you're so persistent…"

I squeezed his hand and my heart raced. My persistence was about to pay off.

"No touching." His face had a look of determination.

I scrunched my forehead. "No touching? What do you mean?"

"Let's keep things above the shoulders, and I guess arms are okay too." He glanced at my hands encompassing one of his.

A laugh attempted to escape my lungs, but I held it in. Was he serious?

"Why?" I asked.

He sighed. "You know what I'm like. I'll give this my best shot, but I don't want it to be physical."

I frowned as the disappointment sank in. Nothing physical? "What about kissing? That's above the shoulders."

He smiled. "Kissing's okay."

"But no touching." I tried to look serious, to let Josh know

I would follow his rules, even though they didn't make much sense. "I don't understand, but I'll do anything you want."

Josh groaned. "Don't say stuff like that?"

"Did you want me to argue with you?"

"No. Just don't say *I'll do anything you want* while we're sitting on my bed. It makes my mind go to bad places."

I wanted to flirt with him, to try to find out more about those bad places, and ideally get him to take me there with him. But I didn't want to mess this up. If Josh was saying no touching, I'd go along with it.

"Sorry." I bowed my head, pretending to be ashamed.

He laughed, then stood, his hand still in mine. "You should get home. I'll walk you out."

"I don't have to leave." I released my hold on him, sensing again that Josh wouldn't appreciate me being too clingy. "I already told my mom I was staying over. It'll wake her if I go home now."

"You're planning to stay the night?" His expression was hard to read.

"Yes, but it's no big deal. I stay over all the time."

It was still impossible to determine what Josh was thinking, but his lips turned down into the hint of a frown. "So, you'll be in the guest room?" He pointed toward the adjoining wall.

I hesitated. I'd found Josh's bed incredibly comfortable. Falling asleep hadn't been my intention, but after convincing myself that he wouldn't mind me waiting here, I'd snuck inside, and the rest was history.

Was there even a microscopic chance he'd let me stay in his room tonight?

"No way, Allie," he said, as if he could read my mind, and

I had to smile because he sounded exactly like Mia. "You sharing my bed is a terrible idea."

"We don't have to do anything."

The thought of snuggling against Josh's chest, maybe even waking up in his arms, made my heart tap dance.

He shook his head, and it wasn't the slightest bit convincing. But I wasn't going to press my luck. Tonight, all my dreams were coming true. There was no need to be greedy.

I reluctantly stood. "Okay, I'll go. But before I do, we should plan our first date."

"Our first date?" Josh ran a hand over his short hair. It looked as if the idea stressed him out, which wasn't a good sign.

"Don't worry. I'll come up with some ideas." I grinned as I wrapped my arms around him, aware I might be breaking his rules with the chest to chest contact, but Josh didn't object. I gave him a firm squeeze, then pulled away enough to kiss him on his cheek before stepping back. "Goodnight."

"Night, A." Josh had a mild look of bewilderment, like he wasn't sure what he'd signed up for. It was hopefully only tiredness, but he had nothing to worry about. This was going to be incredible, and I was going to prove it.

I was giddy with excitement as I left his bedroom. This was happening! I wanted to charge down the hallway to Mia's room, to share my earth-bending news, but she was probably with Ryder, or asleep. I'd tell her everything in the morning.

Instead, I went into the guest room and flopped onto the bed. My mind whirred, thinking of all the new possibilities in my life. It didn't feel real. It hadn't sunk in yet. Josh had never been more than a dream for me. How did I get so lucky?

Even though I was exhausted, the excitement kept me

awake. I was so tempted to sneak back into Josh's room. It was one of my long-standing fantasies, and I might have given it a shot if it hadn't been for his silly rules. Hopefully he'd abandon those sooner rather than later.

My thoughts shifted to plans for the rest of the weekend. Where should we go on our first date? Despite the rules, I still liked physical contact. Mini golf? I imagined Josh standing behind me, his hands gripping on top of mine on the putter as he showed me the correct technique.

Nope. It was still freezing out, and standing in the cold shivering wasn't my idea of fun. Besides, did Josh even have any golfing skills to teach me?

Bowling? Again, he could move in close, show me the right way to glide the ball down the lane, assuming he knew how. Plus, with the shoe rental, it wasn't like he'd be able to change his mind and run away—a fear that lingered in the back of my brain.

Making sure he couldn't escape was the way to go. I mulled it over until inspiration struck. Josh enjoyed fixing things, problem solving. And even though I couldn't wait to spend time with him one-on-one, starting off in a group situation might not be a bad way to gently shift the dynamic between us.

Even though he seemed willing to give me a chance, I'd follow the advice he used with Noah. Making him comfortable was the best route to success.

The more I thought over my idea, the more perfect I decided it was, and as I drifted into sleep, all I could do was hope the rest of the group would feel the same.

25

Josh

IT COULD either have been the scent of waffles or the sound of Allie's laughter that drew me to the kitchen. I wasn't sure which, but either way, my feet knew where to go without any thought requirements on my part.

That was a great thing, because there was a high probability my brain had combusted and I was no longer capable of rational thought. It was the only explanation that made sense to my frazzled mind.

Allie had been low-key flirting with me for years. She'd ramped it up over the summer, but I'd stood my ground. How did she knock down my walls?

I'd given in to her advances, and even though I should've been regretting it, lamenting that Allie had chosen to be with me, instead of someone who deserved her, I was too damn excited.

"Good morning." I strode into the room.

Mia and Ryder probably looked at me, but I only noticed Allie, standing next to the counter, wearing the same clothes as yesterday. Her eyes lit up as she met my gaze, making me feel like a billion bucks. She smiled her happiest smile, and it hit me that we could make this work.

Allie was fun, full of life, and I always had a good time with her. I loved it when she laughed, and when she beamed at me like this.

And even though I wasn't good enough for her, I was apparently what she wanted.

"Are you two just going to stare at each other?" Mia's laugh shook me back to reality.

"No." I scowled, embarrassed to have been caught in the moment.

Allie laughed. "We've been waiting for you. I have an idea for our first date."

The lack of reaction from the others told me that she'd already broken the news of our relationship to them. Mia stood patiently next to the coffee machine while Ryder kept his eyes on the sizzling waffle iron.

"Let's hear it." I took a seat at the table. I'd go along with whatever made Allie happy, so long as it didn't involve roller coasters or other stomach-churning thrill rides.

"I'm not sure what you'll think, because it works best as a group activity. Mia and Ryder have already agreed, and I'm planning to invite Chloe and Nate too, to make up the numbers. I've checked online and there's a place in Brookhill with an open slot this morning, but obviously I wanted to ask you first before suggesting it to Chloe and Nate, and before booking. We can do something just the two of us if you prefer, but I thought this sounded fun, and it's like you said about Noah being more relaxed. So, what do you think?"

I glanced at Mia, and like the best sister in the world who always knew what I needed, she placed a mug of coffee on the table in front of me. Behind the island counter, Ryder plated up the now fully cooked waffle. With any luck, that was headed my way too.

I switched my attention back to Allie, who had a cute look of expectant excitement. "I think you need to tell me what the activity is."

"Oh." She giggled. "Yeah, that might help. It's an escape room."

"An escape room? I've done a couple before. They're fun."

"So that's a yes?" Allie grinned.

I nodded, then took a gulp of coffee while Allie typed into her phone at breakneck speed.

"You hungry, bro?" Ryder asked.

"Always." I moved to stand, but Allie jumped up to grab the plate from Ryder.

"Can I decorate it for you?" she asked.

"Sure, if you want to. Lots of syrup."

"I know." She shot me a smile. Guess I'd spent enough time around Allie for her to have noticed my sweet tooth.

She covered the waffle with what looked like the perfect amount of syrup, then arranged berries in the grooves in a pattern that vaguely resembled a smiley face, but equally could have been an abstract design.

"Thanks, A," I said as I took it from her. "I could get used to this."

"You'll have to let me sleep over more often then." She winked.

That was a bad idea. Whatever was happening between us needed to be at a glacial pace. Most other guys would jump at the chance to have *sleepovers* with someone as sexy as Allie, but I wasn't like that. At least I didn't want to be. Not anymore.

Hence the rules. Clear guidelines to keep myself in check.

Allie's phone buzzed.

"That's a yes from Chloe and Nate," she said. Then, while I polished off my plate, she booked the *extreme horror experience* for us. Fortunately, there would be time for a quick basketball workout before we needed to leave. I had plenty of energy to burn.

"I should go home." Allie stood up with exaggerated slumped shoulders. "I need to shower and get changed."

"I'll walk you out," I told her.

"Thanks."

On the short walk to the front door, we arranged that I'd pick her up in just over an hour, and we'd travel up to Brookhill as a group.

"I'm really excited about us, Josh." She placed her hand on my chest.

Was that allowed? I was the one to come up with the rules, and I didn't even know. But I wasn't about to object.

"Me too."

Her eyes widened at my admission. "Thank you for giving me a chance."

"Sure." I smiled. I wanted to brush off her comment like it was no big deal, but we both knew it was. To me, attempting a relationship was a deal of epic proportions.

She returned the smile and dropped her gaze to my lips. I stepped closer, but Allie didn't kiss me. She didn't even offer one of her *never miss an opportunity to squeeze someone* hugs. Instead, she backed away, out of the door.

I opened my arms to her in question, then dropped my jaw in confusion when she didn't hurtle into my embrace.

Allie grinned, moving farther away. "Not while I'm stinky. I'll hug you later, I promise."

"I'll hold you to that."

She rolled her eyes and shook her head, filling me with satisfaction that she'd understood my joke, even if she thought it was bad.

With Allie gone, I went back into the kitchen, bracing myself for Mia's reaction. Ryder had left the room.

"What are you doing, Josh?" Mia asked the moment our eyes met. "Please tell me you're serious about this. Don't play with Allie's heart."

"I'm not playing with her heart." I glared at Mia, annoyed by the suggestion.

She frowned. "So you actually like her? Like, like her like her."

"Yes, Mia. I *like* her like her."

"You do?" Her lips curved into a smile. "Since when?"

I blew out a breath to convey I wasn't planning on answering any personal questions.

"Well, you guys have my full support," she said. Huh? That was easy. "You can go outside now. Ryder's waiting."

Even though she'd dismissed me, I approached Mia and pulled her into a quick hug. Her support meant a lot, and I felt a pang of guilt that she hadn't expected the same from me when she wanted to begin her relationship with Ryder.

I released Mia from my grasp, then, as a parting gift, I bopped her on the nose. She was never quick enough to stop me, so I left the room chuckling.

Ryder would tease me next, but he'd be happy for us too. Then it would be on to my first date with Allie, and even with the other people there, and the ominous sounding extreme horror experience, I was looking forward to it. I couldn't wait.

26

Allie

"MOM?" I called as I entered the house.

"In here." Her voice came from the kitchen.

"I have a date today," I blurted as I joined her, unable to hold back my amazing news for a second longer.

"Another date?" Mom glanced up at me from the table where she was looking at paint swatches. Yes, again. She was obsessed. "More board games? You like this boy a lot, don't you?"

I hesitated. It had thrilled Mom to hear all about my date with Noah, especially since it involved a potential new hobby. "Yes, I really, really like him. But it's not Noah."

That caught Mom's attention, and she looked up again, this time giving me more scrutiny.

"It's Josh!" My grin erupted. This was the best thing that had ever happened to me, and I wanted to buy a megaphone just so I could let everyone know.

"Mia's Josh?"

I nodded. "I'm so happy, Mom. Josh is amazing."

Mom didn't know Josh all that well, but of course she'd heard a lot about him from me.

She smiled. "Congratulations. You look elated, but remember to keep your feet on the ground."

"I know, I know."

"I mean it. You have a tendency to get carried away. But if you're serious about this relationship, don't rush it. And try to relax a little. You don't want to scare him off."

I nodded. Mom meant well with her advice, but this was Josh. We were already well past the getting-to-know-you stage. As far as I was concerned, it should be full speed ahead. It would be a struggle to hold back.

Mom laughed as I swept her up in an excited hug. Then, not having long to get ready, I dashed up to my room.

I was almost ready on time, but the knock on the front door happened while I was still debating the individual merits of my sweater collection. I wanted to pick the one that most said *touch me*, but I wasn't sure if that would be more driven by fabric texture, or by going with a tight fit.

Out of time, I grabbed the tight pink one, squeezing myself into it while I sprinted downstairs. Hopefully my face didn't drop too much when I opened the door to find Noah, not Josh.

"Hi, Noah?" I said in confusion.

He gave me a friendly smile. "Hi. I'm here for tutoring."

"Oh! Of course, come on in."

In all the excitement, I'd forgotten about the Saturday morning event that would be a regular occurrence until Gavin's grades improved.

"Gavin!" I yelled. Then I turned my attention to Noah, and the guilt took hold.

He'd been fine when we talked yesterday and hadn't appeared at all upset about keeping things in the friend zone.

But to tell him I'd started dating someone else, less than twenty-four hours later? It made me sound horrible. And that it was Josh? Would he think we'd been using him? Had we?

"Are you ready for tomorrow?" Noah asked, raising his eyebrows.

He'd invited me back to the board game club. This time we'd be playing an epic fantasy game, the one that the miniatures in his car were for. He promised the rules weren't as complex as for the first game we played, and he'd suggested I read the rule book in advance so as not to need to trust Big Mick.

"I might have to wing it," I told him through a smile. "Sorry, but I don't think I'll have time to learn the rules."

Noah shook his head at me in pretend disappointment. He was so cute, and even though he wasn't my perfect guy, Noah would make a great boyfriend for some other girl, assuming he wasn't too afraid to talk to her. But he was noticeably more relaxed around me now, and we hadn't really spent a lot of time together, so hopefully it wouldn't take much.

"Noah, there's something I wanted—"

Another knock on the door interrupted me, and this time I knew who was there. I opened the door to Josh, meeting his twinkling eyes. I wanted to launch myself at him, hug him and cover him in kisses, but it felt as if Noah deserved the truth first.

"Hey, man," Josh greeted Noah.

"Hey."

"How's it going? Did Allie give you the update?" He

smiled down at me, making my heart patter. Guess that saved me from having to find a way to break the news.

Noah's eyes flitted between us. "Are you guys together?"

"Yeah." Josh hooked his arm around my shoulders. "I'm sorry for getting you roped into everything." He winced slightly, as if the guilt pained him.

"That's okay. It was good practice for putting myself out there, and you gave me some useful tips that seemed to work." He glanced at me as if hoping for confirmation that he'd been a great date, so I nodded. "And it was fun, even if I was only your puppet." He laughed.

"So, we're cool?" Josh asked.

"Yeah, we're cool." Noah smiled, returning his gaze to me. "And now we have an Elara for game night tomorrow, so thank you. It's always better to have more players."

"I'm looking forward to it," I said truthfully. "You can tell me all about Princess Elara tomorrow."

Noah shook his head with a smile at my assumption. "Not a princess, sorry. But yeah, I can explain some of the lore on the way over."

"Sounds good."

"We should get going," Josh spoke up. "Ryder and Mia are waiting in the car."

"Are you going somewhere fun?" Noah asked.

"We're doing an escape room," I said. "I guess it's a triple date."

"A triple date?" Gavin's voice came from the stairs. "So you guys actually are together? Why did you lie to me?"

"I didn't lie. This is new."

Gavin gave me a look like he didn't believe me, then he focused his attention on Josh. Maybe Gavin was debating whether to give him some kind of protective brother warning, *you make her cry, I'll make you cry.*

Even though it was obvious he wouldn't last long against Josh in a fight, I would've enjoyed the sentiment.

Gavin shrugged. "Whatever. Just be careful of her."

Aww, that was a decent attempt. Gavin did care. I wanted to hug him and tousle his hair, but he'd hate me for embarrassing him.

Josh nodded, tightening his grip around me. I loved it. I loved the feel of his arm holding onto me. It felt protective, maybe even a little possessive.

It was a sign that my instincts were right, and as Josh led me down to his car, only releasing me after opening the passenger door, it was as if a dart of ecstasy hit me.

This was my life now, and although we hadn't even had our first date yet, I already had great hopes for the future.

A future with the guy I'd always wanted.

With Josh.

27

Josh

"ANY FINAL QUESTIONS before you go inside and get locked in?" Trent, our Game Master, asked. He looked to be around mid-twenties with a scruffy beard, and he had his enthusiasm level set to super-high, possibly even higher than Allie's. He'd already sat us down and completed a long speech, explaining the rules of the game, and had stressed several times that we would be safe inside the room, even if we were afraid.

Chloe spoke up. "Do you know the fastest time for this room?"

"Forty-two minutes and twelve seconds."

She exchanged a smile with Nate, who nodded. Guess escaping wouldn't be enough for them. We'd need to do it in record time.

"Well, I think you're all set. Remember that I'll be watching and listening, so if you need a hint, just ask."

There were time penalties for hints that got more severe with each use, so things would need to get desperate before we were likely to give in and ask for any.

Trent grinned with almost devious excitement as he

opened the door and watched us walk inside. He didn't lock the door behind us for safety reasons, but if anyone left the room, they wouldn't be allowed back in, and there were no refunds.

The room was a standard rectangular box shape. There weren't any windows, so the only light came from the ornate floor lamps—one in each of the four corners—which each had different color bulbs: red, blue, green, and a soft white.

A large digital clock above the door lit up, and our hour countdown began.

"We need to do this methodically," Chloe said. "Nate and I will start clockwise from the door. Mia and Ryder go counter, and Allie and Josh take the back wall. Anything movable that looks like a clue gets put on the desk, then we'll see what we can do with them. Okay?"

No one put up an objection to Chloe taking charge, so we split into our respective couples.

Allie took hold of my hand, then led me over to the far wall. We'd held hands before—when leaving the warehouse after her date with Chris—but I'd acted on impulse and it hadn't even really registered.

This time I was aware of everything. Even though I liked the warmth, the daintiness of her slender fingers linked through mine, being connected to another person this way was a strange sensation. It was all completely foreign.

I'd already tried to act natural by putting my arm around her at her house, but I didn't know if that was right. I didn't know how to be a boyfriend.

Allie dropped my hand as if taking it hadn't been a big deal at all, so I shook away my doubts, forcing my concentration onto the puzzles ahead.

While the other walls were covered by an assortment of pictures in frames, along with an overbearing bookcase, our wall only had one giant poster. That and a door.

The door drew my attention first. There was a license plate sign screwed on which read *Bravest*. Beneath that, at waist height, was a metal flap which could be lifted to reveal a hole in the door. To the side, a keypad was attached, suggesting that we would need a four-digit code to unlock the door and hopefully escape to freedom. The only clue for us to decipher was the poster, which was an illustration of the night sky, including labeled constellations.

I stared blankly, waiting for inspiration to hit.

"Any ideas?" Allie asked.

"No. I don't know anything about stars. Do you?"

She shook her head. "I wish I did. I love them."

Allie looked at the poster with enough awe that anyone might think she was stargazing for real. I fought the urge to pull her to my side, to plant a kiss into her hair. In a room full of couples, the last thing we wanted was for the PDA to start.

Without a puzzle to solve, we returned to the center of the room where there was an old-fashioned mahogany desk, sitting all alone in the middle.

So far, our group had gathered up a few clues. There was a book with the writing on the spine upside down, *from outer space*, and a small, locked box missing its key. But of most interest to me was the wire with alligator clips on its ends.

"Another wire," Mia announced, pulling it from a hollowed-out book and forming a collection on the desk.

I glanced around the rest of the room, looking for any circuitry I could attach the wires to, but there was nothing.

We spent the next few minutes searching for any clues that

we might have missed on the first pass over the room. Nate found another wire behind one of the picture frames on the wall, but we didn't turn up anything else.

"The colored lights must mean something," Ryder mused.

"I think they're in order," Chloe said. "And that it somehow links up with the colors in these pictures."

Mia shrugged. "The lamps go around in a circle. How can it be an order if we don't know where it starts?"

"There must be something that tells us where to start," Chloe answered. "Or maybe we need to switch certain ones off."

Nate dropped his head into his hand, letting out a gentle laugh of frustration. "That was what I suggested ten minutes ago. The bluest picture has a cross on it."

Chloe laughed. "You should have suggested it a little louder." She took hold of Nate's hand and guided him over to the lamp with the blue bulb.

"They're so funny," Allie said, looping her arm through mine. "I think they enjoy arguing with each other."

"You don't like to argue?" I raised my eyebrows.

"No. I much prefer getting my own way with no resistance." She grinned, and there was a mischievous spark in her eyes.

"No, you don't."

"Yes, I do." She giggled.

I could keep it going, make her laugh some more, but wary of crossing into annoying territory, I let my joke end on a high.

"Let's figure out the book," Allie said, releasing my arm so she could retrieve the book with the upside-down spine from the desk and bring it back to me.

While the rest of our group ran around in circles attempting to solve the mystery of the lamps, Allie and I stood next to the white one and read through the book together. It was an allegedly non-fiction account of an alien invasion on earth, which for something so ridiculous was a surprisingly engaging story.

Maybe we could have done more to aid our escape, but there had to be something significant in the book, and we were making it our mission to find it.

"Look." Allie pointed ahead on the page and read aloud. "They claimed their location in the galaxy would be revealed only to the bravest."

In the margin next to the passage, someone had scribbled the numbers 8632.

Allie grinned at me with excitement. "The keypad!"

"Did you guys solve a puzzle?" Ryder asked from where he stood on the desk, waving a UV flashlight over the ceiling tiles on Mia's instruction.

"Yes!" Allie darted to the door. She waited there for me with impatient eyes.

"Go ahead," I told her. "8632."

She typed the numbers in, and the door clicked unlocked.

"We did it." She clapped then gave me a quick one-armed hug before pushing the door open and stepping inside.

I followed her into the darkness, and a voice—that of our Game Master, Trent—crackled out from a speaker above our heads.

"The bravest have entered!" He cackled, playing it up for drama. "The room is one-way only, so once you're inside, you can never leave!" Then, at a reduced volume, he added, "Unless you find a way to escape in the next twenty-seven minutes. You're ahead of the curve. Awesome job, guys. Oh, and please shut the door."

Nate had been about to join us in the room, but he stilled in the doorway and smirked. "Guess you two are the bravest. It was good knowing you." He pulled the door closed with a chuckle.

"It's so creepy in here." Allie clutched onto my arm with one hand and flailed at the wall with the other. "I can't find a light switch."

"Don't worry. I'll protect you." I leaned my head down to kiss her hair the way I'd been wanting to for the previous thirty-three minutes.

"I know." I could hear the smile in her voice. "Just, this was supposed to be a horror experience, and so far…"

"You think there might be something scary in the pitch-black room where only the bravest are allowed to enter?"

"That's what I'm dreading. But how can we even do anything in here when we can't see a thing?"

My mind scrolled through multiple things we could do together in the dark, but I refused to be controlled by temptation. And even if I was going to cave—which I wasn't—this was the wrong time, and definitely the wrong place for anything to happen between us.

I pushed my rampant thoughts away. My focus should be on solving puzzles and easing Allie's fear. And for that, we needed light.

As if by magic, we got it when someone lifted the metal flap on the other side of the door, letting in a stream of illumination. It was faint, but better than nothing.

"You guys okay?" Ryder asked.

"Yeah, but we can't see anything. Have you finished with the flashlight?"

There was some scrabbling from the room, and then Ryder pushed the flashlight through the hole in the door. I took hold and switched it on using the standard LED setting, then I swung the light around the room.

On one wall was a grid of metal pins. Perfect. A home for the wires. The opposite wall was obscured by text. Individual unconnected words in white marker, some the right way up, others written upside down.

A group of people stood at the back of the room. Not real people, but life-sized models, mannequins. One was a standard green alien statue, and the others were covered up, wearing hooded cloaks.

Allie gripped me tighter as the beam of light passed over them.

"Just pretend they aren't there," I told her before talking through the hole in the door. "We're going to need all the wires."

Someone pushed them through to us.

"What's in there?" Chloe asked.

"There's a circuit board. A big grid. I can use the wires to connect it up. To make a shape."

"The constellations," Allie said under her breath.

"What shape?" Chloe asked.

"It has to be one of the constellations on the poster," Allie answered. "We just don't know which."

I waved the flashlight over the words on the wall. "The answer must be somewhere in this room. The book said the location would be revealed to the bravest."

"You don't think we need to turn off the light again, do

you?" Allie squeezed my arm harder. "To prove we're the bravest."

It was worth a shot. The answer might be written in glow-in-the-dark pen.

"You ready?" I asked.

"Nope, but let's get it over with."

I laughed, plunging us into darkness for only the time required to see that wherever our clue was, it wasn't going to be found glowing on the wall.

Or was it?

"I have another idea," I said, switching the setting on the flashlight to UV.

Bingo.

The light wasn't strong enough to cover the wall, so I stepped closer until I could sweep the flashlight over it. Some words glowed. Constellation names I recognized, mostly from staring at the poster. I moved along until one word stood out. Cassiopeia. It was the only one that was upside down, just like the spine of the book.

"You're a genius." Allie twisted to face me, then she pressed her soft lips against mine.

Yeah, I could get used to this. I ached to deepen the kiss. It was the first time our lips had touched this morning, and I was hungry for so much more than I could have right now.

Later. I'd kiss her again later. I reluctantly pulled away from Allie, and switching the flashlight back to the regular LED setting, I knocked on the door. The flap opened.

"It's Cassiopeia," I said. "What does it look like?"

There was a moment of silence, then Mia answered. "It's a W. A tilted, squashed W."

Right. I remembered that one. It was the easiest shape

from the poster, but would I be able to recreate it? As I straightened the wires in my hand, the answer became clear.

"Guys, we need another wire," I called through the door.

"We still have the locked box," Ryder said. "I bet it's in there. But we can't find the key."

We'd ransacked the first room, and my gut told me that the key wasn't out there.

Because it was in here.

I blew out an apprehensive breath, then shone the flashlight over to the end of the room.

"Don't go near them, Josh." Allie clung to my arm like she thought we were in mortal peril.

But going over there was the obvious solution, so I braced myself, and then I stepped forward.

28

Allie

JOSH TOOK a step toward the figures at the back of the room, as if he had no survival instinct at all, and as if I wasn't physically holding him back—or at least trying to.

"Are you coming with me?" he asked with amusement.

I gulped and dropped his arm. Something about the dark hooded figures was putting me on edge, even more than dark hooded figures normally would.

"I think there's someone breathing over there," I said, my heart pounding against my ribcage.

Josh laughed in response and took another step forward. "Look." He pointed the flashlight at one of the figures, or more accurately, at the thick gold chain hanging around its neck. "Are you thinking what I'm thinking?"

Considering I was thinking about how disappointing it would be to die a virgin, probably not.

Josh walked right up to the figure wearing the chain. I froze. I wouldn't put it past him to fake a scare, just to get a reaction from me. He would do that to Mia for sure, but he wouldn't do it to me. Would he?

My heart thudded faster as Josh tentatively stretched out his arm. Then he did the most stupid thing.

He switched off the flashlight.

"Josh!" I shrieked. "Turn it back on."

Silence.

The flap on the door opened, and I jumped a mile into the sky. The hole provided a tiny amount of light, but glancing over toward Josh, I couldn't make out a thing.

"What's happening in there?" Mia asked.

"Josh is trying to scare me. Tell him to put the flashlight back on."

Mia laughed. "Do you think he'll listen to me—hey!"

The flap closed, forcing me into complete darkness once again. Did someone pull Mia away? Maybe the horror experience was back in the first room, and everything in here was only a distraction.

"Josh?"

He ignored me. I sucked in a deep breath, filling my lungs, then releasing the air slowly.

There was nothing to be worried about. Live actors were a staple of horror experiences, and Trent had gone on and on about how we would be safe even if we were afraid. It must have been to protect any actors, because working in this environment, it would be easy for them to become victims of self-defense.

And as for Josh trying to scare me? I was expecting it. I was expecting him to jump out with a *boo!* any second, and if I was expecting it, there was no reason to be scared.

"Josh?" I repeated. "Where are you?"

He answered my question by grabbing hold of me, then pushing me back against the wall with a slight thud. He moved so fast, there was no time for fear before excitement took over.

Josh pressed his lips against my mouth, then kissed me slow and deep.

Tingles sparked through my body, warming me from inside out. The kiss was firm, controlled, and it was everything I'd been waiting for. Now wasn't the time for reckless passion, but knowing he'd been thinking of me too made my heart patter with anticipation. He hadn't changed his mind about us.

This was only the beginning.

My fingers stroked over his neck and up into his hair. I couldn't get enough.

My moment of bliss only lasted a minute before the door flap opened again. Josh pulled his head back but kept me in his embrace.

"Are you still looking for the key?" Chloe asked.

"We just found it." Josh pulled the chain from his pocket and passed it through the hole.

"Don't go anywhere." She snickered. "I'll unlock the box."

Josh returned to my lips for one more sweet kiss before he switched the flashlight back on.

"You scared me, you jerk." I slapped at him, letting my hand come to rest against his chest. I loved touching him, but would he push me away?

Josh laughed, leaving my hand where I'd placed it. "I'm sorry, A. I couldn't resist. Will you forgive me?"

I pursed my lips. "Hmm, I'll try, but I expect you to make it up to me later."

"Oh yeah? I'll have to think about how to do that." He

rubbed his chin, but the dark look in his eye told me he was having ideas I was certain I'd enjoy.

If Chloe hadn't chosen that moment to push the wire through the door, I would have done my best to get Josh to tell me what he'd been thinking. But as it was, he caught the wire and wasted no time in getting to work.

He gave me the flashlight to hold while he attached the alligator clips to the board with a confidence that suggested he remembered the constellation shape a lot better than I did.

"Are you sure that's right?" I asked. He'd stepped back from the wall as if to say *job done*, but nothing happened.

"I'm fairly sure it's wrong." He chuckled. "Guess we need help from outside."

Instructions regarding angles and orientations flew through the hole in the door the second we asked for them. Josh seemed to understand what they meant, and it only took a few minutes to get the star pattern correct.

A pre-recorded message played when he connected the final wire and completed the circuit. "Congratulations, you have solved the puzzle. Your escape route is at the back of the room with the bravest. Gather your belongings and make your—"

I screamed, pointing the flashlight at the shrouded figure which had advanced on us while I wasn't paying attention, and was now less than five feet away. The figure lunged forward, forcing my pulse to skyrocket as the fear struck me.

Josh didn't miss a beat. Before I had time to blink, he positioned himself between me and the figure. His arms were out to the sides, reaching back in a protective stance. "You okay, A? He won't hurt you."

I put my hand over my heart, feeling the rapid pounding while I caught my breath.

"—don't touch the actors, and they won't touch you," continued the recorded message.

The actor took a step back.

"Allie?" Josh reached his right hand farther behind him until he touched my hip. Because of his stupid rules, I'd expected him to pull his hand away, but he didn't.

He gave my hip a gentle squeeze, then shifted his hand up to my waist, holding it there with a steady grip, despite the awkward angle. Even though I'd been wishing for Josh to touch my body, these weren't the sensual, hungry caresses I'd been longing for.

Instead, his actions were comforting, letting me know I was safe.

"I'm sorry. I can be a little jumpy."

The door to the first room swung open to reveal Chloe. "The timer's still running. We need to escape."

Josh released his grip on my waist as Chloe stepped into our room, holding Nate's hand. They strode through with carefree determination, all the way to the exit door beyond the figures. The actor tried to scare them by waving his arms forward and back, but they pretty much ignored him. I felt so foolish for my fear.

Chloe stopped by the door. "Come on, what are you waiting for?"

Josh twisted to face me, then he glanced down at my hand, almost in consideration. He picked it up, linking his fingers through mine. My heart's rhythm was still stabilizing, and this contact was another setback in that regard.

I wasn't sure how he felt when I took his hand earlier, since he'd looked a little surprised. But this was such a couple thing to do, and it was getting me too excited. Like we were going to be a normal couple and do normal couple things.

I loved the feeling of safety that came with holding his hand. I trusted him to protect me, even though my rational brain knew I didn't actually need his protection right now.

"Use me as your shield," Josh said.

I grinned. That just made him even more heroic. Like he was volunteering to sacrifice himself for me.

Josh gave a gentle tug on my hand, then led me past the actor who had frozen still as a statue. Guess he was good at that. Mia and Ryder followed behind us. The actor lunged at them as they passed. Mia flinched then burst into laughter.

Nate opened the exit door, and we poured out into the bright fluorescent hallway where Trent was waiting.

"Congratulations, guys. Forty-three minutes on the nose. Awesome job."

"Forty-three minutes?" Chloe's face dropped, and Nate pulled her into a side hug. "We were so close."

Trent laughed. "It was a valiant effort, so try not to lose sleep over where you could have made up the forty-eight seconds. Some people took things more seriously than others." He theatrically arched an eyebrow and glanced at me and Josh in a way that was so obvious that everyone else looked at us too.

Was Trent watching when Josh kissed me in the dark? It would make sense for them to have night vision cameras. I bit my lip, a tiny bit embarrassed. Not that I would have skipped that moment for anything, even if it meant breaking the room's record. Sorry, Chloe.

Josh shrugged, and he dropped my hand. "I thought we did well to find the door code."

Trent nodded. "Yeah, you did. That's the part that most often slows groups down. They don't always look through the book carefully enough."

Josh met my gaze with an almost proud smile. We worked well as a team.

After taking a group photo and saying goodbye to Chloe and Nate, Josh drove us back toward Haven Valley. A victorious sensation swirled in my stomach. Not only had we won the escape room, but I'd won the life I always wanted. I'd finally won over Josh.

His kisses left me breathless, and it was impossible to describe the feeling of safety, of security that rushed through me every time Josh demonstrated his protective instincts.

Mom had warned me not to get ahead of myself, but I couldn't help it. There was only one word to describe what I felt for Josh.

Those four letters that sent me free-falling.

Love.

29

Josh

ALLIE SWUNG OPEN the front door and ran down toward my car as if she'd been watching for me, which she most likely had.

Our relationship was moving at full throttle, way faster than I'd intended. I should've been playing it cool, backing off instead of encouraging her, but I couldn't get enough.

I already felt dumb for resisting for so long, for missing out on the way my heart reacted to her adoring smile, and to all the sweet kisses.

"Hey." Allie entered my car and leaned over to kiss my lips.

Sweet kisses exactly like that.

"I can't believe you want to do this." She grinned, and it was probably because she knew she was the main reason why.

"I figured I'd give it a chance. Ryder assures me it's fun."

"It will be, especially now that you'll be there."

My lips curved into a smile. She had to stop saying stuff like that before I got an inflated sense of self-importance. Not that it was a bad thing. A contrast to the way I usually felt.

I'd spent all weekend with Allie. After leaving the escape room, we'd gone back to the house and hung out as a group. To be honest, I was glad for the extra company, because Allie's tight pink sweater had been calling out *touch me*, and her lips had been saying *kiss me* all day—both metaphorically and literally.

Ryder had cooked some romantic dinner for Mia, so I took Allie out for burgers—her choice. We went back to Jimmy's since it was hands down the best place around. After a couple of hours, we returned to the house, and that was when Allie invited herself up to my bedroom. She used the excuse of giving Ryder and Mia some privacy while they watched an awful high school movie.

It must have been Mia's pick since it starred an actor who looked a lot like a younger version of Ryder. Pretty pointless when she had the real guy sitting next to her.

Upstairs, Allie pounced on me like a tiger, telling me how much she'd been waiting for this. The feeling was mutual, but even though my body was aching for more, we kept our lips and hands to the safe zones. She didn't break the no touching rule, which was a relief, because I was way too weak.

If she tried to seduce me, I wouldn't have been able to resist.

Allie had reluctantly gone home last night, only to be back again this morning. It should have been too much. Too much, too soon.

But it wasn't. And even now, I'd delayed driving back to the dorms until the last minute, just so I could spend as much time with her as possible. At least Ryder encouraged the change of plans too. I wasn't the only one in over my head.

And even though I still didn't really know how to be a boyfriend, I was muddling through, and Allie didn't seem to have any complaints.

She chattered away while I drove, telling me about all the tabletop games she'd played last week, and about Noah's miniature models that sat on his dashboard.

Allie sure knew how to fill the silence, but I loved listening to her. There was no droning; she was way too excitable. She'd even reacted with avid interest this morning when I explained my forthcoming hot dog experiment, and she made me promise not to do it without her there to watch. It was such a small thing, but it meant a lot to me.

We arrived at the board game club to find Noah waiting in his car for us. He climbed out, carrying the miniatures that Allie had described.

"Hey, man. Thanks for letting me tag along," I said.

"Are you kidding? Big Mick is thrilled to have another player."

We followed Noah into the back of the store, and he introduced me to Mick.

"And this is Ashley," Noah said, his cheeks reddening as he glanced at the girl sitting to the side of Mick. She had cropped jet black hair, which I was pretty sure was not her natural color, heavy eye makeup, and a stud in her nose.

Was Noah crushing on this girl? Not who I would've expected him to go for at all.

Ashley smiled at us, her eyes lingering on Allie, studying her with an almost curious expression.

Mick gave us an overview of the game. It was co-operative, with all five of us working toward a common goal. I got the feeling we were only here to make up the numbers, and that we'd be given plenty of instruction on the best moves to make on our turns.

My gut feeling had been spot on, although as the game progressed, I got the hang of things.

Under the table, Allie rested her hand on my knee. I shot her a warning glance, and she reacted to it with an innocent smile. Pushing her hand off me wasn't something I wanted to do though, and so long as she didn't try to inch higher—which surely she wouldn't—I guess her touch was okay, even though it made concentrating on the game a challenge.

"How did the escape room go?" Noah asked, speaking up about something other than game tactics for the first time. "It looks like you made it to freedom."

"Yep," Allie answered. "It was fun, although terrifying. Josh and I solved the main puzzle. We had to go into a dark room, and after finding the clue for a star constellation, we recreated the shape on the wall to complete an electrical circuit." She squeezed my knee.

"Cool. What constellation?"

"It was the one that looks like a squashed W."

"Cassiopeia," Noah said with a smile.

Allie grinned back. "Are you into Astronomy?"

He nodded. "My grandparents gave me a telescope for my birthday. I'm fascinated by it, and cosmology."

"Really? I never would have guessed that. Chloe loves cosmology too."

"Oh," Noah raised his eyebrows. "Yeah, she's excellent at physics."

Allie bit her lip in slight confusion, and it was all I could do not to pull her toward me and kiss her. She had to be getting mixed up with cosmetology, because I was sure Chloe was more into makeup and beauty science than the origins of the universe.

Correcting Allie might have embarrassed her, but I wanted to wipe the confusion from her face. Under the table, I threaded my fingers through hers, still on my knee.

She glanced over at me with a smile.

"Stargazing's weather dependent," Noah said. "But you're welcome to join me sometime. Everyone is." His eyes swept over Ashley, and he continued looking around the table until his gaze ended on mine.

My lips tightened into a knowing smile. Noah had barely said anything directly to Ashley all night, and she'd been quiet, too. Talking to Allie hadn't given him the practice he needed to ease his anxiety, but if there was anything I could do to help him, I would try. It was the least I could do.

Not that I'd have any advice specific to Ashley. It had been so much easier with Allie, because I already knew her so well. I already knew what would make her happy on a date.

Mick cleared his throat. "The universe is fascinating and all, but we have a warlock on the loose here on earth."

We went back to the game, but even though I was following what was happening, it wasn't gripping my attention. At least not as much as Allie's actions under the table.

She lifted our hands, moving them over and then down to rest on her knee instead of mine. It was the perfect moment for me to have pulled away, but of course I didn't.

I tried to listen to Mick counting his attack points, but my mind was too distracted by the way Allie dragged our hands a few inches up her thigh. She wiggled her fingers free, leaving my hand on the middle of her thigh, on top of the denim fabric.

What was she playing at? I glanced over, and this time, I was faced with a vixen. She had a flirty smile, like she was daring me.

Allie wanted me to explore higher, and I wanted to just as much, probably more. But putting me in this situation didn't help my resolve. She knew we weren't supposed to be touching, so I shot her a stern glare and pulled my hand up to the surface, to the tabletop, and to safety.

Allie frowned, and the disappointment on her face hit me harder than I expected. It was the face of rejection, something I knew all too well.

The last thing I wanted to do was make Allie feel like that.

"Yeah!" Mick cried out as he high-fived Noah across the table.

Ashley rolled her eyes at him, but she had a grin. "Great game, guys."

It was over? Allie looked as confused as I felt. No, it was more than that. The confusion was only masking the hurt on her face. She smiled, and I doubted anyone else noticed it was forced.

"Mick got the amulet for twenty points, giving us an instant victory," Noah explained.

"Nice job," I said to Mick. "That was fun, but we should probably get going. Do you want any help with packing up?" I stood.

Noah shook his head. "We can handle the tear down. Thanks for coming, though. The game's so much better with more people."

"Sure," Allie said. "I'm not convinced we did much to help, but I enjoyed it." She gave Noah a warm smile, but she remained sitting at the table.

"Are you ready to go?" I asked.

Allie glanced up at me, then her eyes flipped to Noah. Did that mean she wanted to stay?

She hesitated for long enough that my heart raced. Then she stood and slipped her hand into mine. "Ready."

I swallowed my doubts as I gripped onto her, said goodbye to the others, then led her back out the side door we'd entered through, and into the chilly winter air.

"Are you okay?" I asked.

She nodded, looking down at her feet. "I'm sorry. I shouldn't have—I know you don't want to get physical."

I groaned. Then, acting like a caveman, I pushed her back the few steps we'd moved from the store until she was up against the wall.

"Don't you get it?" I stared into her startled, yet excited, eyes. "I want you *so* much, A. Too much." I dipped my head and kissed her hard, as if my words needed to be proven. I moved my lips to her slender neck and murmured against her skin, "That's why we have the rules. I can't control myself around you. And when you touch me, or get me to touch you, I don't know how to resist."

Allie reached her hand to my face, stroking her smooth fingers over my rough chin. "But I want you too. You don't have to resist."

I backed away from her. It was the only thing I could do that wouldn't end in me dragging her into the backseat of my car and doing everything I craved.

Allie frowned. "I'm sorry. You're right. I—I don't get it."

Guilt hit me. "Allie." I pulled her into a hug as the tension inside evaporated. "Let's just take things easy. I'm giving you everything I can. Isn't that enough?"

Was this it? Was this the moment she'd tell me that *no*, it wasn't enough. I wasn't enough.

She pulled away to study my face. "You're everything I ever wanted. The past two days with you have been incredible."

I didn't know what to say, so I took her hand and led her to my car, driving her home and resisting the urge to do more.

"I don't want to get out," she said, giving me a helpless smile after I stopped the car outside her house. "It feels like I'm not going to see you for months."

I laughed. "I'll be back again first thing Saturday morning."

"And we can spend the day together?"

"Yes. The entire weekend."

A huge grin broke across Allie's face. "I can't wait."

"Think about what you want to do."

She nodded with enthusiasm but made no move to exit the vehicle.

"Get out of here." I chuckled.

Allie blew out a dramatic sigh, then she unbuckled her seatbelt and leaned over to me. I supported the back of her head as she gave me a tender kiss goodbye. This was what I needed. Not clothes flying around the room in a fit of passion, but something sweet, gentle. Full of love.

I pulled away. That word had no place near me.

"I'll see you Saturday, Josh. Thank you for an amazing weekend."

Allie didn't wait for me to respond before leaving my car.

She ran to her front door, then looked back and waved before going inside.

I stared at her house for a minute. All the lights had been off, suggesting Allie was home alone.

If I went to knock, there was no doubt in my mind that she'd welcome me inside.

It was tempting. Way, way too tempting.

30

Allie

THANKS TO HER DANCE TRAINING, Mia had bucket loads of stamina. I, in contrast, only had one bucket. And it was a little leaky.

It wasn't unheard of for us to hike multiple laps around the mall, searching for that one elusive item that was exactly what Mia sought. She had a unique determination to find whatever it happened to be, and at least it ensured I got enough exercise.

Today, I intended to tap into her drive for my own purposes. Not being as meticulous with my clothing choices, I didn't do it often. But whenever I needed to find the perfect item, Mia was an invaluable resource.

"Help me pick out something Josh will like." I tugged on her arm, which was looped with mine, and guided her toward the lingerie store.

"From there?" Mia stopped still and her usually pretty face contorted as if the suggestion horrified her.

It probably did.

"I just want to be prepared."

Mia glanced at me and cringed. "Is he pressuring you? You don't have to rush—"

"No." I sighed heavily. "It's the opposite."

"The opposite? Don't tell me you're pressuring *him*?" Mia's eyes widened like she found the idea of Josh needing encouragement utterly preposterous. That just made me feel worse.

"I'm not trying to pressure him. I just want to tempt him a little. He says he doesn't want to get physical."

That's what he said with words, but his actions, his kisses, and the way he looked at me, all made me believe otherwise.

"Allie, that's awesome."

"Awesome?" I scoffed. "It doesn't feel awesome. I know he's been with other girls, but I'm supposed to be his girlfriend. Why am I the one missing out?"

Mia let out a soft laugh. "Firstly, I doubt you're missing much. And secondly, don't you see what this means? He's treating you differently. It shows he's serious about you. That he respects you."

My heart lifted. I wanted so badly to believe her words were true, that I was special to Josh. But it was a struggle when it felt like he was holding back.

"You don't think he'd respect me if we had sex?" I asked.

"I didn't mean it like that. I just don't think you have anything to worry about. Remember, he's never had a girlfriend before, and Josh can be closed off. It isn't easy for him to let people get close."

I nodded as a pang of sympathy struck me. Even though Mia was trying to tell me not to rush the relationship, all she was doing was making me more determined. I needed to get close to Josh. To give him the love he deserved.

It was like there was a hurdle in front of us, and it was

only on the other side that Josh would truly let me into his heart.

Mia squeezed my arm against her side. "I still can't believe you wore him down and made it this far."

I smiled. We'd been together for less than a week, but every time I thought of Josh, the warm fuzzies took over. It was still hard to believe he was giving me a chance. That he'd admitted he liked me too.

"Will you help me then?" I pleaded. "So that if the opportunity arises to take it further, I'll be ready."

Mia gazed at the lingerie store, her expression unable to hide her apprehension.

"I thought you'd enjoy the mission," I said. "Find me something sexy, but classy, not trashy. Unless you think Josh would prefer trashy?"

Mia wrinkled her nose in disgust. "I don't even want to think about—" She shook her head. "You don't need my help with this, and I'm sorry, but it's too icky. Would you want to pick out sexy underwear to help Gavin's girlfriend turn him on?"

Gross. As far as I knew, Gavin didn't have a girlfriend, but her analogy helped me understand why she was refusing to help.

I sighed. "Fair enough, but I still want to buy something."

"You can. I just don't want to see, okay?"

I nodded. It was a shame Chloe wasn't with us. She'd have had no problem offering opinions, but she had plans with Nate today. His mom wasn't supportive of their relationship—in her warped mind Chloe's family wasn't good enough—so whenever she was out for extended periods, Chloe didn't miss the opportunity to go to Nate's house.

"How about I go get some nourishment?" Mia suggested. "You can meet me up there when you're done?"

Nourishment referred to food court burritos, her kryptonite. With a nod, I agreed to meet Mia later, then I entered the high-end store alone. My eyes roamed around, imagining all the possibilities.

I wasn't going to force myself on Josh, but I wouldn't hold back either. I wanted to get over that hurdle, and if I could tempt him, seduce him somehow, then I would.

31

Josh

THE FRONT DOOR swung open in front of me.

"Hey, man." Gavin's eyebrows lifted. "Allie didn't say you were coming over." He stepped aside to let me into the house.

"She doesn't know."

Allie was so damn excitable, that once I had the idea of surprising her, I hadn't been able to shake it. I wanted to hear her squeal with delight and let her knock me to the floor while flying into my arms.

That was why I'd neglected to tell her I'd be back in Haven Valley tonight, over twelve hours earlier than the expected Saturday morning arrival.

"Go on up," Gavin said. Then, with a slight smirk, he added, "I'll stay out of your way."

"Thanks, bro."

Outside Allie's bedroom, I took in a deep breath, then rapped four times on the wooden door.

"Yeah?" she called.

I pushed open the door and took a tentative step inside. Allie wasn't in sight, but the door to her closet was open.

"Please don't tell me that because Mom's out you think you can have your creepy friends over."

Despite the irritation in her voice, it was like a siren's call, drawing me closer, until I stood blocking her exit, trapping her in the closet.

That was when she turned around to face me.

"Josh!" She squealed the way I'd imagined she would, and as predicted, she launched herself in my direction. "I can't believe you're here! Why didn't you tell me?"

I laughed, returning Allie's hug, before prying her off me. "I thought this way would be more fun."

She grinned. "I usually hate surprises, but I'll let you off just this once."

"I don't believe you hate surprises."

"Okay, I love surprises, so long as they're good."

"Do I count as a good surprise?"

"What do you think?" She reached up toward my face with both hands, even though she was holding something black and lacy in one of them.

Then, as if realizing, she pulled back her hand and bent her arm behind her back, while simultaneously leaning in to plant her lips against mine.

Was she trying to hide something from me?

Even though I'd been dying to kiss her, my curiosity needed to know, so I ended the kiss before it had really started. "What have you got there?"

Allie bit her lip, looking down like she was embarrassed, and I fought the strong urge to kiss her again.

"I've been underwear shopping." She brought her arm back in front of her body, showing me the lacy black bra she was clutching. "What do you think?"

Speechless, all I could do was stare, not even bothering to pretend I wasn't imagining what she'd look like wearing it.

"I thought you might like it," Allie said. "But I'm not too sure it's me. Why don't I put it on, and you can give me your opinion?"

Hell no. She wasn't offering to model for me. That was too bold. Even for Allie.

The fingers of her free hand played with the bottom hem of her t-shirt, as if waiting for the go-ahead before getting changed.

"Allie, no. We agreed we weren't going to—"

"We agreed no touching. But you can look, right?"

She lifted the hem a fraction of an inch, giving me a glimpse of the smooth skin of her stomach.

Even though I'd seen plenty of Allie's body during the summer days beside our pool, this was different. Teasing, and only for me.

I wanted to step forward, to strip her clothes off her myself, but instead I swallowed the lump in my throat. "I'm not going to look at you wearing sexy underwear."

"So you like it? You think it's sexy?" Her eyes twinkled. "Let me try it on for you. I can tell you want to see."

"No." I grabbed hold of her wrist, holding her loosely, but firmly enough to prevent her from shedding any clothes, which I was almost positive she'd been about to do. "Don't tempt me."

She tilted her head to the side and gave me a sweet, yet defiant smile. "Maybe I want to tempt you."

Damn. She was putting in a valiant effort.

"Why?"

She hesitated, and her smile tipped down ever so slightly.

"Well, because you're super-hot, and when you touch me it's like there's a surge of electricity and I feel like I'm going to explode. I'm like one of your hot dog wieners."

I couldn't hold back my laugh, and I released my hold on her wrist, no longer worried she was going to strip.

Allie's smile picked up. "I know we're new, but I hate it that there are girls out there who know you better than I do."

What? She was jealous? I'd never pegged Allie as the jealous type, but what she was saying made sense. I should have realized.

"Not better, just different." I hooked my finger under her chin, then lifted her head up. "I can't undo the past. But trust me. You already know me way better." I pressed my lips softly against hers.

Allie sighed into me. "I want to know you better in every way."

Unable to think of an answer that would satisfy, I kissed her again, keeping things slow and steady while my brain struggled to fight against my heart and my body.

Allie pulled away. "Let's go into my room." She opened a drawer and stuffed the black lace inside. I wished I could see everything else she had in there. Taking my hand, she led me through to her bedroom. To her bed.

She left me there while she closed the door to the hallway and switched off the overhead room lights. We still had some illumination from the bright bulb in the closet, casting a yellow glow over the room.

A jolt of adrenaline hit me. Had Allie misunderstood my intentions? Did she think I'd agreed to get to know her *in every way*?

That should have been a bad thing, but I didn't want to correct her, and the thought sent my pulse racing.

She sat down next to me on the bed. "I know you don't want to get too physical…" *Wrong.* "But I haven't been able to stop thinking about you, and so I was hoping we could make out for a bit? I'll obey the no-touching rules."

A smile tugged at my lips. Allie was so cute. What the hell had I been thinking with those rules? I wanted to touch her everywhere.

"Forget the rules." I pulled her toward me.

She didn't hesitate to return my enthusiasm, kissing me back with an excitement that made me eager to give her anything she wanted. And the more she kissed me, slipping her fingers under my t-shirt and stroking over the muscles in my back, the more I believed it was possible.

That I actually could give her everything.

My lips moved to her neck, kissing and nibbling, while my hands explored the contours of her body through her clothes.

Allie squirmed underneath me, then she tugged at my t-shirt, pulling it up, letting me know she wanted it off.

I complied, shifting away from her body for only as long as it took to strip off my shirt, before finding her hot mouth again. I kissed her deep and slow, keeping things controlled for as long as I could manage.

But it didn't take much before my control waned and things turned frantic. The voice in the back of my brain told me to relax, but I wasn't listening, because there was a more pressing problem to solve—Allie was wearing way too many clothes.

"I want this off," I told her, gripping her top in my fist.

"Okay," she breathed out, then scrambled to peel it off over her head without hesitation.

And though I would have enjoyed seeing the lacy black bra hugging her skin, the revelation of the innocent soft lilac fabric—with an even lighter polka dot pattern—felt more true to her personality. She was beautiful, exactly as she was.

Allie looked up with a self-conscious, nervous kind of smile that I wasn't used to seeing from her. My heart hammered in response. She was amazing, perfect. She deserved so much better than me.

Don't think like that.

I banished my doubts. Allie wanted this, and I cared so much for her. This had to mean something.

She stared up at me with enough longing to make me feel like a king.

"It doesn't have to be tonight, Josh. But whenever you're ready, I want you to be my first."

Damn. I forgot how to breathe.

Allie grinned, then pulled me back down, kissing me with a white-hot intensity that set all my nerves aflame. She eroded my self-restraint until I didn't know how to resist anymore.

And I didn't want to.

32

Allie

"ARE YOU STILL OKAY?" Josh had a lazy grin as he slipped back under the covers.

My breathing had stabilized, but I still couldn't quite believe that this was my life. That I had an amazing boyfriend. One who didn't seem to mind the way my eyes had followed as he'd paraded butt-naked across my bedroom to the wastebasket and back. One who I'd fallen for with everything I had.

He was all mine.

I nodded, returning his smile. "I'm still okay."

"Good." His dark eyes sparkled as he leaned over and placed a quick kiss onto my forehead, before lying down next to me.

Josh must have asked if I was okay a thousand times. Not enough to annoy, but exactly the right amount. He'd made everything about me. Making sure I was comfortable, despite the awkwardness, and taking things slow until I insisted he didn't need to hold back. I loved him for it.

I twisted onto my side, then ran my fingers over his chest.

He was so perfect. Strong, but soft too, not a solid wall of muscle.

Josh's warm brown eyes gazed at me. Then, without warning, he pulled my body on top of his. I let out a small yelp, then couldn't hold back my giggle. We were both still naked, and even though the idea of going again sent a rush of excitement through me, I wasn't sure my body could handle it.

"I love the feeling of you against me," he said, low and quiet, like it was a secret admission.

"Me too."

He kissed me. Grazing his lips over mine in a way that brought back all the tingles. It was tender and loving, and everything I wanted.

I smiled against his lips.

"What are you thinking?" he asked.

"Just that…" I hesitated. Was it too soon?

"Tell me." Starting from my mouth, he trailed a finger over my cheek, and then down my neck.

I took a deep breath. I'd never said these words before, at least not in the romantic way. "I love you."

"What?" Josh paused the movement of his finger and his thick eyebrows lifted as if I'd completely shocked him.

I swallowed the lump in my throat and tried again. "I'm head over heels in love with you, Josh."

He didn't react at all, so I waited, staring into his eyes, watching as they clouded over.

My heart sank. *Oh crap. It was too soon.*

"Allie, I…" His lips twisted into a frown, and I could picture the gears turning in his head.

"You don't have to say it back," I said, rushing the words, but the damage was done.

"I'm so sorry." Josh lifted me off his body, discarding me to the side, and even though his hands were gentle, it felt like a cold, hard shove. "This was a mistake."

My heart pounded. What was happening?

"I never should have—damn, I'm sorry, Allie." He slipped out of bed, gathered his clothes that were scattered across the floor, then began to dress, not even looking at me once.

"Are you being serious right now?" I shifted in the bed, about to go to him, but stopped, aware of my nakedness. I never usually felt vulnerable around Josh. But I did now. It suddenly felt like he was someone else. "Josh. Talk to me."

Was this all my fault? He hadn't wanted to get physical, but I'd coerced him anyway. Josh had made it clear he wanted to move slow, but I pushed him. And now I'd told him I loved him after just a week. After just two days spent together as a couple. I was such an idiot.

Josh glanced over at me with dark, unemotional eyes. "This should never have happened. Any of it."

Any of it? Our whole relationship?

"Are you kidding me?" Tears pricked behind my eyes. "I just told you I love you and now you want to break up?"

"It's for the best. It'll never work between us. You can't love me, A."

I gawked at him. *What?* How dare he tell me who I could love.

A flash of sympathy passed over his face. "I don't want to hurt you, but—"

"A bit late for that, isn't it?" I gave him my most murderous glare through the tears pooling in my eyes. "I can't believe you used me, you jerk!"

He stared at me, as if in shock. But I'd given myself to

him, body and soul, and he'd smashed up my heart. He didn't deserve to look surprised.

"You're just as bad as Chris, and all the guys you tried to keep me away from," I said, getting control of my voice, even though the tears were escaping and trickling down my cheeks.

Josh stepped toward the bed, his face full of guilt, like he actually felt bad about it. "Allie, I—"

"Don't come near me."

He came closer anyway.

"I mean it, Josh. Get out!" I grabbed for the only chuckable thing I could reach.

"I'm trying to pro—"

Mr. Giraffe bounced against his chest. I'd hurled the toy with all my strength, but it was too heavy and cumbersome to go far. At least it stopped Josh from advancing any closer.

If he tried to touch me, I'd disintegrate.

"Okay." He held up his hands in surrender. "I'll go. We can talk tomorrow."

"No. I don't ever want to see you again." The fake concern on his face made me angry. "I hate you."

Josh swallowed as if my words had somehow affected him. But he was heartless, so that wasn't possible. He glanced down at the floor, then without saying anything, or looking back, he slipped out of my bedroom.

And out of my life.

33

Allie

THERE WAS no way I was leaving my bed. Josh could hammer on the front door as much as he wanted. I wouldn't let him back in. Ever.

He'd crushed me. Squished me like a bug.

And I'd let it happen. Worse, I'd made it happen. Mia had been warning me away from him forever, but I refused to listen. Even when Josh shared the crude inner workings of the male brain, I'd thought he was talking about other guys. But he was the same.

The hammering downstairs stopped, and an unwanted wave of disappointment hit. I was such an idiot to feel this way. A part of me wanted him to persevere, for it to mean he thought I was worth it. That he wouldn't give up, because he loved me after all.

I sniffled and cuddled Mr. Giraffe tight. Picking him up from the floor was all I'd managed before retreating into the warm safety of my bed. It was the worst place for me to be though. All I could think of was Josh, and what we'd done here together.

But I'd still be remembering that no matter where I was. There was no escape from my mind.

Someone knocked hard on my bedroom door, causing me to bolt up in surprise.

Mom was on a date tonight, and the last time I saw Gavin he'd been planning to go out too. Was he still here? Had he been here the whole time?

"Who is it?" I called out, wrapping the bed covers around myself to provide some modesty.

"It's Mia. Can I come in?"

Mia was here. My heart skipped a beat as I realized I wasn't all alone in this.

"Yeah, come in."

The door pushed open, and Mia stepped inside before halting. Her mouth dropped open, and she just stood there, gaping at me. I hadn't even thought about how awful I must look. Josh had roughed up my hair, and I was pretty sure my lips were swollen, but it would have been all the sobbing that accounted for how ugly I was.

Gavin pushed through Mia. "What happened?" His wide eyes trailed over me and darkened. "You're naked? Did Josh—" He seemed too stunned to say anything more.

I collapsed my head into my hand, unable to maintain eye contact. This was so embarrassing. I didn't want Gavin knowing anything about my sex life—even though it was already over. And the thought that he might've been home the whole time I was with Josh made me nauseous.

Mia sprang into action, taking hold of Gavin's arm and driving him toward the door with gentle authority. "Leave it to me. She'll be okay."

Gavin didn't react. All he did was glance back, gawking in shock until Mia shut the door with him on the other side.

She rushed to the bed, sitting down on the edge. "Oh, Allie, what happened?"

There was so much love and concern in her voice that I burst into uncontrollable sobs again. Mia wrapped her arms around me, holding me until I calmed down.

"What happened?" she asked again. "Did you and Josh…?"

I nodded, and despite everything, my stupid lips wanted to smile at the memory.

Mia frowned, a worry line appearing on her forehead. "He hurt you?"

I shook my head. He didn't hurt me, at least not physically. "He was so amazing, Mia. I know you don't want to hear the details, but it was amazing. It was everything. He made sure I was okay, and I… I hate him." I sniffed, grabbing another tissue from the nearly empty box beside my bed.

"Um, I'm not sure I'm following. Why do you hate him?"

"Because I messed up. I ruined everything."

"*You* messed up?" Mia looked at me like I wasn't making any sense at all.

I nodded, then choked out, "I told him I loved him."

"Oh." She gave me a sympathetic frown, like she knew where this was going. "I'm guessing he didn't say it back?"

"No. I don't think I expected him to, but I wanted to tell him. I wanted him to know."

"You think he got scared?"

"I don't understand what happened. One minute he was being super sweet, and the next… it was a complete one-eighty. He said it was a mistake. As in, *we* were a mistake. He doesn't want to be with me anymore." I blew my nose, but it didn't help.

Mia clenched her jaw. "I'm going to kill him."

"No, don't. It's my fault. I knew he didn't want to get physical, but I pushed him anyway. And he never wanted to be my boyfriend, but I forced him. He wouldn't even kiss me until I... I should have listened to you. I'm so dumb."

"You're not dumb."

"He doesn't care about me at all."

"That's not true. If he didn't care, he wouldn't have called me. He told me you needed me, and he was really upset. I could tell."

"He called you?"

"Yeah." She gave me a half-smile. "Why did you think I was here?"

I shrugged. I hadn't given it any thought.

"You should get dressed," Mia said. "Maybe take a shower. It might make you feel a little better."

That seemed unlikely, but Mia was trying to help, so I reluctantly agreed. She went downstairs to make hot chocolate, leaving me alone to drag myself out of bed and into the shower.

And as I washed away the last traces of Josh, I tried to make sense of things.

It was impossible.

Tonight had been shaping up to be the best night of my life. But instead it turned into the worst.

How did it go so wrong?

34

Josh

ALLIE HATED ME. But not as much as I hated myself.

I slammed my car door. I'd been planning to drive and drive until I reached the end of the world, but my autopilot brought me home.

There wasn't any reason to go inside the house, so I skulked around the back, past our pool—covered up for the winter—and to the wall-mounted basketball hoop.

Ryder was there, waiting under the floodlight, and when he saw me, he bounced the ball in my direction. We played in silence, just shooting hoops.

Even though it was freezing out, I knew he'd stay until I told him to leave. Or until I was ready to talk.

Eventually, the words wanted to come out. I took possession of the ball, then collapsed against the wall. "I couldn't resist her."

Ryder sat down next to me.

"I tried, but I couldn't do it anymore. I'm so weak, bro."

"You're human."

Barely human. More like a monster. I'd shattered her heart, seen the pain in her eyes. All caused by me.

"Isn't that what Allie wanted, though?" Ryder asked. "From what Mia said, it sounded like she was on a mission to get you into bed."

I let out a dry laugh. "Mission accomplished. But I made a huge mistake."

His face twisted in confusion. "You guys weren't safe?"

"Of course we were." I shot him an annoyed glare.

Unprotected sex was too risky, even though I was clean. I'd gotten tested before winter break, hoping to get close to the girl I'd crushed on for most of senior year. But even though Jennie had been up for some fun, I turned her down. In the end, she hadn't been who I wanted.

But a pregnancy? That would be a disaster. Having kids wasn't even something I could imagine years in the future. I'd make an awful father.

"So what went wrong?" Ryder asked.

I ran my numb fingers over the dots on the basketball. "She told me she loved me."

Her confession had floored me. It felt like the best news and the worst news, all wrapped up in one.

"Wow, already?" He glanced over. "You don't feel the same?"

"I can't give her what she deserves."

Ryder frowned, and I could tell he was deciding whether to argue with me, so I continued talking.

"Besides, it's not like she meant it."

"You don't think she meant it?"

I was almost positive she thought she meant it, but she was wrong.

"I'm not lovable." I gripped the basketball harder in my hands and stared down at it. Ryder had to already know, but I'd never said it out loud.

"What?" His shock was obvious, even though I couldn't bring myself to look at him. "You don't actually believe that do you?"

With a sudden urge to get away, I pushed myself up from the ground.

Ryder jumped up after me, moving to block my path. "Bro, wait. I'm sorry, I didn't realize you felt... but it's not true, and if Allie says she loves you, you should believe her."

I shook my head. "How can anyone love me when not even my own parents do?"

Ryder's jaw dropped, and I had to look away. "You don't think they love you?" His voice was deathly serious.

I turned to face him with a scowl. "What do you think?" I trusted Ryder. Would he lie to me?

He scratched at the back of his neck. "I don't know. I hope so, but they sure don't show it."

I nodded. The trust was still in place.

"But that's on them," he continued. "They don't show it with Mia either. You think that means they don't love her? That she's unlovable?"

I shrugged as if it didn't matter, even though it did. But our parents always preferred Mia, so it wasn't the same.

Ryder shook his head. "She's definitely lovable. I love her. And please don't repeat this, because I don't want to start any rumors that I take after my dad, but I love *you*, too. You know that, right? And so does Mia."

"Thanks, bro," I let out a low chuckle, appreciating his

attempt to lighten the mood. But then my mind latched onto what he said. "You love Mia?"

"Yeah, I do."

"Have you told her?"

"No. She wants to take things slow, and I don't want her to think that because I've said..." He trailed off. "We were talking about you and Allie. Now I've set you straight that you're lovable, are you going to give her a chance?"

Ryder was my family. Him and Mia. They were the only people I could ever let myself believe loved me, and Ryder could say I was *lovable* until he was blue in the face, but it wouldn't make it true.

Except...

No. I was too conflicted. Nothing made sense. And even if I might've had a chance with Allie, I'd blown it now.

"It doesn't matter anymore," I said, jogging over to the hoop and swishing the ball through the net. "Allie hates me."

"Yeah, she does," came a voice from out of the darkness. "And so do I."

I froze, waiting while the voice advanced toward us until I could see who was there. Allie's brother, Gavin.

He was flanked by two friends on each side, and all five of them carried baseball bats.

Oh shit.

Ryder moved to stand next to me in a united front, and a rush of adrenaline surged through my veins. These guys were younger than us, and pretty scrawny too. It would be two against five, and even with the baseball bats, we could probably take them.

But I couldn't fight. Allie would never forgive me if I hurt her brother, and Mia would never forgive me if anything happened to Ryder.

I swallowed. Maybe I should surrender and let them beat me. It was what I deserved.

Gavin stepped forward, slapping the baseball bat against his open palm. In the cold air that had to sting, but he didn't even wince. "I let you in."

"What?"

"I can't believe I let you in." He was seething.

I didn't know how to react, so I just stood and watched as Gavin's friends caught up with him, stepping into formation.

"I know what you did." He glared at me with pure hatred, and I couldn't even blame him. I'd broken her heart. I knew it. I'd practically heard it snap.

He took another step toward me, cracking the bat into his hand. "You raped my sister."

Wait. What?

"And now you're going to pay."

35

Josh

RAPE?

My mouth went dry. That he thought I could... Why would he think that? Did Allie tell him...?

I was going to throw up.

"You've got the wrong idea," Ryder said. "It wasn't like that."

"Were you there?" Gavin asked, scowling at Ryder. "Because I saw what state he left her in. It doesn't take a genius to connect the dots."

Guilt took over. I knew she'd be heartbroken. That was why I made that quick call to Mia. But to be so distraught that her brother thought I'd forced myself on her?

"You aren't going to deny it?" Gavin pointed his bat at me. "Claim you never laid a finger on her?"

I stared at him, unable to talk. Unsure what to say.

Half of me wanted to set him straight, while the other half wanted him to come after me with the bat.

"It was consensual," Ryder told him. "You need to talk to her."

Gavin ignored Ryder and glared at me. "Deny it. I dare you."

He was fuming. I could see the anger building behind his eyes, sense it from the way his knuckles turned white where he was gripping the bat.

I found my voice. "I didn't rape her."

"You expect me to believe you?" he snarled.

His friend on the far right snickered. "Beat him, Gav."

"I'd never hurt her," I said, focusing on Gavin, even though I felt like such a fraud. I had hurt her, and we all knew it. Just not in the way he thought.

Allie didn't deserve the way I treated her. She was incredible. She was perfect. If things were different, if I were normal, it would be so easy to admit my feelings. Even if only to myself.

I took a breath. "I—I love her."

"You love her?" Gavin repeated, and for the first time, there was doubt in his eyes.

"Yeah, I do." I stood tall, staring him down. The words had fallen from my mouth, but as I said them, I knew they were true.

"What are you waiting for?" the annoying friend sneered.

Gavin kept his eyes locked on mine. He was wavering.

Ryder pulled his phone from his pocket. "I'm calling Mia."

"He'll call the cops, get him!" the annoying guy yelled.

"Wait." Gavin held his bat out to the side, blocking his friend's path, even though he hadn't advanced an inch. "I want to hear what Mia says."

We stood in tense silence while Ryder waited for Mia to answer the call. My heart thumped as the seconds ticked by, and my hope that she'd answer slipped away. Until she did.

"I know, I'm sorry," Ryder said. "It's important. We have a situation here. Allie's brother showed up with some friends." He glanced at me. "They think—they think Josh raped her."

Mia's outraged reaction was loud enough for me, and doubtless the other guys, to hear. She babbled something indiscernible, and then Ryder held out the phone to Gavin. "She's going to get Allie."

Gavin eyed the phone with mistrust, then stepped close enough to grab it. Close enough to take a swing at me if he wanted to. I stood my ground.

"Allie?" Gavin stared at me while he listened. "Calm down —for real? But you—" She cut him off, and I wished I could've heard what she was saying. "No. We haven't done anything to him."

My heart gave an involuntary thump. Even after what I did, Allie was worried about me.

"Yeah, okay." Gavin's gaze was still fixed on me, but his expression was softer now. It wasn't a smile, but I could see the relief there, in place of the anger. He ended the call.

"Well? What did she say?" one of Gavin's friends asked.

He glanced back. "It was a misunderstanding."

The sneery friend thumped his bat against the ground in annoyance.

Gavin handed Ryder his phone, then he hesitated, looking at me again. "I'm sorry, man. I honestly thought that—"

"I get it. We're cool." I understood his reaction, and if I ever thought someone had touched Mia without her wanting it, I would've behaved the same. Worse.

He nodded, then turned and made a hasty exit with his friends.

"You meant it, didn't you?" Ryder asked as soon as we were alone. "You love Allie?"

I shook my head. "It doesn't even matter. I've ruined everything."

"I bet it would matter to her. You should tell her."

"No. It's too late. It's already over."

That was as much as I needed to say. Ryder wouldn't argue or try to convince me that things were salvageable. Not yet. But Mia would want to express her opinion, and I didn't want to stick around to give her the chance.

"I'm going to go back to the dorms," I said.

"Right now?"

"Yeah. Before Mia gets back."

I could already imagine the way she'd yell at me for breaking her best friend's heart. And even though I deserved it, I didn't want to hear it from her. Not now. I couldn't take it.

Ryder nodded. "I'll drive."

"What? No, you don't have to come with me."

"I don't mind." He was trying, but he couldn't hide the concern on his face.

"Seriously, Ry. I'll be fine. And no offense, but I want to be on my own."

"You sure?"

"Positive."

"What can I tell Mia?" he asked, stopping me from walking away. "You know she's going to ask for your side of the story."

I hesitated. "You can tell her the truth." It didn't matter anymore. I was tired of pretending. "Just not that I…" I couldn't finish, but I didn't need to. Ryder understood.

Inside the house, I grabbed my bag from where I'd

dumped it next to the front door. I didn't even make it upstairs earlier. I'd been way too excited to rush over to surprise Allie.

My heart hammered as I remembered the taste of her lips, the feel of her body melded with mine. But it was all over. I'd destroyed everything, the one perfect thing in my life.

She hated me, and that was what I deserved.

36

Allie

"I CAN'T BELIEVE I never realized you had a crush on Ryder," I said, forcing a smile and shifting my gaze from the TV to Mia. "Alex Redwood could be his twin."

Mia laughed, her eyes fixed on the teen heartthrob. We'd watched all of his movies together over the years. Some were better than others, but mostly they got worse and worse.

Mia had suggested watching a light-hearted movie to cheer me up a little, to help take my mind off Josh. It was an impossible task, but I was trying, and teasing Mia was a minor distraction.

"Who did you like first?" I asked.

"Ryder, for sure."

"So that's why you liked Alex Redwood? Why you forced me through all his movies? So you could imagine it was Ryder?"

"Hey, I didn't force you. You liked him too, remember?"

I shrugged. "He's a hottie." He was totally cute, but he didn't even come close to Josh.

Mia smiled, then froze at the sound of the front door opening.

Was that Mom? Even after showering, slipping into my coziest pajamas, and curling up with a hot chocolate and an awful movie, I was a mess. Last time I checked, my eyes were red and my face was blotchy. It would be obvious I'd been crying, but I didn't want Mom to know. There was no way I could tell her the truth about what happened tonight.

She'd warned me not to move too fast, but I'd ignored her advice and had done this to myself.

Gavin entered the living room, and I let out my breath. He'd already seen me much worse than this, and the way he'd reacted warmed what was left of my heart.

I jumped up from the couch and scooped my arms around my little brother, who towered over me. "I can't believe you threatened Josh."

"You're not mad?" He pushed me away from him.

I shook my head. My first panicked thought had been concern for Josh, but that went away once I knew he was safe. Gavin wanted to protect me. He was on my side. He did care, and that meant the world. "You were looking out for me. Thank you."

He gave me a small smile, which I could tell he was restraining. "I'm so relieved he didn't... but what happened tonight? You looked awful earlier."

"It was nothing. I was upset because I thought Josh cared about me more than he does. But it's all over now."

Gavin furrowed his brow and bit his lip, as if contemplating something.

"What is it?"

He ignored my question. "So, you're okay?"

"Yeah, I'm okay."

That was a lie. I wasn't okay yet, but I would be. Just as soon as I forgot about Josh…

Gavin gave me another half-smile. Then, after flicking his eyes to Mia, who was staring at the TV and fiddling with her fingers, he went upstairs.

Yes, I'd be okay as soon as I forgot about Josh. Only problem was that I didn't want to.

"I THINK it's time I threw a party," Mia announced to our table at lunch. She was only talking to Nate and Chloe though, because even though I was sitting at her side, I was more like a ghost.

I'd always considered myself resilient, but five days after my life changed forever, the ache was still there. It wouldn't go away.

I was floating through life. I didn't know what I was doing. What to do.

Because I still didn't understand.

Why did Josh pull away?

Did I truly mean nothing to him?

"A party sounds good," Chloe said, and Nate nodded.

"Allie?" Mia glanced at me.

"Count me out for this one. I'm still not in the party mood."

Mia frowned. "I'm not sure I've ever had a party without you there. We'll wait until you're feeling better." She patted her hand on my arm.

Feeling better? Nothing made me feel better. I'd spent all weekend in bed, wallowing in misery. Thankfully, Mom was out most of the time, and after requesting solitude, Gavin had stayed out of my way too.

I'd eaten a whole carton of chocolate brownie ice cream, but not much else since then, and I didn't want any food now, either.

I stood. "I think I'm done with lunch."

Mia's gaze dropped to my barely touched chicken salad. "Do you want me to come with you?"

"No. I'll be okay."

I left the cafeteria alone, keeping my eyes on the gray tiled floor. I was so sick of seeing all the happy couples everywhere. They all had what I wanted.

What I once thought I had.

Hold it together.

Exhaling, I took my phone from my pocket. No new messages. Josh had cut me off dead. I hadn't heard anything from him. I'd briefly considered reaching out, but what was the point? He wouldn't answer me.

Not when he wasn't even responding to Mia. She was relying on secondhand information from Ryder, but she'd promised me she'd get answers. That she'd get through to Josh eventually. And I would wait until she did.

Because I wasn't a quitter. And even though I hated Josh, I still loved him too. And the need to fill that empty void in my heart kept me going.

I would never give up.

37

Josh

MIA HAD SENT ME A 911, an urgent call for action. Until now, I'd been avoiding her calls and leaving messages unanswered. I wasn't ready to talk. I still had no way to explain myself.

But I couldn't ignore her now—she needed me.

She'd driven up to the dorms and then summoned me to the room I shared with Ryder.

I barged inside, relieved to see my sister sitting alone on my bed, unharmed, staring at her tablet. "What's the emergency?" I was short of breath.

"Video call." She smiled and gestured for me to join her.

"What?" I sat down on the end of the bed. "I thought you were in trouble."

"I'm sorry, but you've been ignoring me. What else could I do?" She shrugged, then scooted down so that she was next to me. "I wasn't sure how long it would take you to get here. We still have a few minutes."

"A few minutes until what?"

"Until the video call." She smiled with excitement.

My breath was still coming out heavy. I'd sprinted to get here. "Video call?" I shook my head. "No way. I can't face her. Not after what I did."

Mia's face twisted into a slight scowl. "Not with Allie. With Mom and Dad."

I raised my eyebrows. She'd set up a meeting with our parents?

Her expression softened. "Ryder told me you don't think they love you. Is that true?"

"What do you think, Mia? Honestly." I straightened my face, ridding it of all emotion as best I could.

"Of course they do! It breaks my heart to think you don't know that." Mia hooked her arm over my shoulders.

I blew out a breath, but I couldn't look at her. "What's the plan?"

"We're going to have a heart-to-heart. All four of us."

"I don't have anything to say."

"Let me do the talking then." She gripped her arm tighter around me, as if she thought I was about to up and run away. "Please, Josh. We need this." Mia gave me a hopeful smile.

I doubted a video call would do much for me. Was it even possible to fix our fractured relationship? But Mia wanted this, so I'd stick around for her. I'd at least try.

"And then after the call, we'll talk about Allie," she said, her eyes trained on my face.

The thought of talking about Allie made me sick to my stomach. It was worse than the tornado-coaster, and even worse than the building anticipation of having a *heart-to-heart* with my parents.

"Okay," I muttered. I couldn't avoid it forever.

"Great. Now, get comfortable. They'll be calling any minute."

We waited.

After eight minutes, Mia let out an annoyed sigh. "I can't believe they're late. I spoke to Mom. I told her how important this was."

I shrugged. Just because it was important to Mia, it didn't mean our parents gave a damn. How didn't she realize that yet?

Another five minutes passed, both of us staring at the clock on Mia's tablet in anxious silence. Each time Mia sighed, signaling her hopes deflating more, my anger built.

"I told her," she said, her voice full of anguish. "I told her it was important. That you needed them. She promised me, Josh. She promised."

"Hey, she probably just forgot. You know how scatter-brained Mom can be."

"Mom, sure. But it would have gone straight into Dad's calendar."

I couldn't argue with that, and I didn't know what to say, so rather than letting out all the anger and frustration, I kept my jaw clenched shut. Dad had most likely added us to a spreadsheet. In a hidden column.

"I'm going to send a reminder." Mia opened the messages app.

MIA

We're both here for the call. Where are you?

It swooshed away, into the abyss. Then, less than a minute later, a reply popped up on the screen.

MOM

So sorry, baby. We bumped into some old friends. Call you tomorrow XOXO

Mia must have read it more than once because she was slow to react before flipping the cover over the screen and tossing the tablet to her side.

"I think you're right." She scrunched up her face in a pre-waterworks attempt at being strong. "They don't love us."

I shook my head in sad agreement, then hugged her close. "I hate them for doing this to you."

It was so unfair. Mia didn't deserve this, and now she was coming around to my way of thinking. I'd been trying to persuade her otherwise, but maybe it was futile. She needed to accept the truth, like I already had.

"Doing it to me?" She pulled away, then dabbed at her eyes with the back of a finger. They were damp, but she wasn't crying yet. "It sucks, but I'm okay. I'm happier than I ever have been now that I have Ryder. I'm more worried about you."

"Mia, I'm fine. I'm over it."

"Stuff like this cuts deep, Josh. Did you tell Ryder you were unlovable?"

I sucked in a breath, twisting my head to stare at the door. I ran here because I thought Mia needed me. Not for a therapy session.

"You can't honestly believe that?" she continued. "Because it's not true. Not at all. I love you so much. Seriously. Even though you can be annoying, you're the best brother in the world." I didn't need to look at her to know that the tears were on the loose. "Ryder loves you too. And... so does Allie."

I closed my eyes. I was the absolute worst. I hated myself so much for hurting Allie.

"Talk to me." Mia's warm hand gripped mine. "Why would you say you're unlovable?"

I sighed. "I can't explain it. It's just a feeling in my gut. Like I don't deserve love."

"Josh!" She flung her arms around my chest and squeezed me tight. "You are such an idiot! You're wrong. You're so, so wrong. Of course you deserve love!"

"Mia, stop."

"No." She clung on. "You need to know. Your thinking is all messed up."

Mia cried against me for what felt like forever, mumbling words of concern and uplifting encouragement.

Eventually, she released me, studying my face with wide watery eyes that brimmed with sympathy. "You're self-sabotaging."

Damn. If she kept looking at me like that, I was going to cry too. And I'd grown a thick skin. I couldn't even remember the last time I cried. But self-sabotaging?

"It's not like that."

"Of course it is. Why else would you push Allie away?"

I hesitated. "I'm trying to protect her."

"Protect her? You broke her heart."

"You don't think I know that?" I snapped, not even meaning to.

Mia frowned. "She's been a wreck. A shell of her normal self."

I pushed myself up from the bed. I couldn't take it.

"You need to talk to her."

"I can't. Allie needs to forget about me."

"She blames herself."

"What?" I gaped at Mia. This was all on me. None of it was Allie's fault.

"You know Allie's always had low self-esteem. Talk to her, Josh. Please. Tell her how you feel. She loves you."

"Stop saying that." I paced along the length of my bed. "She deserves so much better."

"Don't be stupid. She deserves whatever makes her happy. Don't you want Allie to be happy?"

I stopped pacing to glare at Mia. "You know I do. That's why—"

"Great. So you'll talk to her?"

"I—I wouldn't know what to say."

"Tell her the truth. Even if you don't want to get back together, please make her understand she didn't do anything wrong."

I nodded. Allie needed to know how amazing she was. But get back together? Mia said it like it was actually an option. Like it was my choice.

"And if you apologize…" Mia lifted her eyebrows, giving me a hopeful smile. "Allie's very forgiving."

"Not that forgiving."

The way I'd trampled over her, I wouldn't blame her for never even speaking to me again. But my heart still flipped at the suggestion.

Mia sighed, and it felt like she was disagreeing with me. "Promise me you'll talk to her."

"I promise."

It was what I needed to do. Because staying away, knowing she was hurting too, probably even more, was tearing me up.

I'd talk to Allie, and I'd tell her anything she wanted to know. I'd tell her everything.

"THANKS FOR THE ESCORT," Mia said as we came to a stop next to her car.

She'd been planning for us to meet Ryder for dinner after our non-existent video call. But instead, wanting to hide her red eyes from the public, we all stayed at the dorms and had Chinese takeout instead.

It was only a short visit—all for me, apparently—and Mia and Ryder hadn't even had any time alone. Not that I would've noticed if they'd started making out in front of me. I'd been too deep in thought all evening.

When it came time for Mia to leave, I walked with them down to the parking lot. Most of the lights were broken, so it wasn't even an option to send her alone into the dark. But now that I was here, I realized it was unnecessary. She didn't need me when Ryder could protect her from any dangers that were lurking.

Mia jingled her car keys in her hand and smiled at Ryder. "I'll see you tomorrow night?"

He nodded, and she turned to me. "Will I see you too?"

"For sure."

She grinned, then pulled me into a hug. "You deserve love, Josh. Remember that."

I flashed her a quick smile as she let me go. She'd been telling me the same thing over and over, like she thought she could drum it into me until I believed it.

Maybe it was working.

I was feeling optimistic. But I wasn't going to get ahead of myself. I'd felt this way before, only for reality to drag me back down again.

Mia turned her attention to Ryder next, diving into his embrace and pressing her lips to his.

I glanced away, my gaze going straight up. It was a clear night, and bright sparkling stars littered the dark sky. Was Cassiopeia visible?

I'd never given the universe much thought before, but maybe I should download an app, find my way around the Milky Way.

Mia and Ryder ended their kiss, so it was safe to look again. Mia hopped into her car, then waved as she drove off.

"You've changed your mind about going back to Haven Valley?" Ryder asked.

"I need to talk with Allie."

He gave me a knowing smile. "Have you thought up a grand gesture?"

I frowned. "A grand gesture?"

"Yeah. Before I made up with Mia, Allie explained grand gestures. She suggested something like a serenade." He raised his eyebrows in amusement. I'd heard Ryder's singing voice, and it was bad. Not that mine was any better. "If you want Allie to forgive you, do something special for her. I'm positive that's what she'd want."

There seemed little chance of her ever forgiving me, and I didn't deserve for her to. But Allie needed to know she was incredible. She needed something to boost her self-esteem. And if I could do anything to make her feel special, then I would.

38

Allie

BY FRIDAY, I was fed up with moping. Josh had been consuming my thoughts all week, but it needed to end. I couldn't continue like this.

Had he even thought of me twice?

"Let's do it," I said to Mia as we stood in the hallway after lunch.

"Let's do what?"

"Your party idea."

"Really?" She smiled. "You feel up to a party?"

"Yes." *No*, but I would try. "Just no truth or dare."

She laughed. "We only ever play that when you suggest it."

I guess that was true. But my dares always revolved around kissing, and I couldn't stomach the thought of kissing anyone again.

I only want to kiss Josh.

I breathed out a heavy sigh, and Mia arched an eyebrow.

"Let's do it tomorrow," she said. "I'll get the word out."

I nodded with fake enthusiasm. Ryder would be back for the weekend; I was sure of it. But what about Josh? Would he come back too? He'd usually always make an appearance at Mia's parties if he was home. And with Ryder in attendance, surely he'd show up too.

Unless he was avoiding me. But he couldn't avoid me forever. Not when I was best friends with his sister. I still hadn't attempted to contact him. I didn't want to sound desperate. Besides, what could I even say?

"Allie?" Mia asked. "Are you okay?"

I bit my lip. "I was just wondering…"

"Yes, he'll be home. He promised he would talk to you. Apologize. Explain himself."

"Oh." I swallowed.

Was I ready to talk to Josh? What if his explanation was that I was a big disappointment? Did I want answers if he left because I was bad in bed? Or because he never even cared about me at all? Was he only with me out of pity? Because I kissed like a toad and couldn't find a boyfriend on my own?

No. I refused to let myself believe that.

"Don't worry." Mia pulled me from my thoughts again. "Just hear him out, and then if you don't want to see him, we'll kick him out."

Her support put a smile on my face. "We'll kick him out of his own home?"

"Yes. If that's what you want. At least out of the party."

"Thanks." I gave Mia a quick hug. She was a great friend.

"So, what shall we do? Small and casual, or a bigger crowd?"

Smaller would be easier at such short notice, but that meant being surrounded by couples, and that wasn't my idea of fun.

"Bigger." I widened my lips into something I hoped resembled an excited smile. "I can't wait."

Mia gave me a kind smile in return, as if she could see through my act. She no doubt could. I wasn't good at hiding my emotions, since I never normally tried to. I preferred to be upfront about what I was feeling, whatever I wanted.

"Bigger it is." She pulled out her phone, and seconds later, mine beeped. I'd be one of many people getting the same message.

Mia had so much freedom to do whatever she wanted. I'd heard plenty of comments about how lucky she was, but most people didn't see the cost. What she was missing out on.

"Has your mom still been calling?" I asked.

Mia sighed. "It's already less, but more than before. We were supposed to have a video call last night, but she couldn't make it."

"I'm sorry. That sucks."

"Yeah." She shrugged. "It was worse for Josh. I feel so bad for him…" She trailed off, then looked at me, a flash of guilt passing over her face.

"It's fine. I feel bad for him too. Even after everything."

Mia smiled and linked her arm through mine as we walked toward our next class. "You're amazing, you know. Not everyone would be so understanding."

I tried to be sympathetic. I'd witnessed Mia's sadness when her parents failed to show up for things important to her, and just because Josh seemed tough on the outside, it didn't mean he wasn't affected by that too.

But understanding?

How could I be understanding when I didn't understand anything at all?

MOM WAS HOME early and already working on a mood board in the kitchen when I got back after school. She opened her mouth to gape at me the second I made it into her line of sight.

"Did you go to school like that?" she asked, her tone both accusatory and concerned.

I glanced down at my outfit, which consisted of dark jeans and a gigantic baggy loose knit sweater in black. The sweater engulfed me and was cozy enough that I remembered why I'd kept it, even though—like most of my clothes this week—it came from the dowdy pile.

I normally took much more pride in my appearance, but this week it hadn't seemed important, and I didn't have the energy. Looking pretty had never really helped me before. Why would it matter now when I wasn't even trying to attract any guys?

Mom frowned, inspecting the rare sight of my entirely makeup-free face. "Is this about Josh? He really got to you, didn't he?"

She gestured for me to come in for a hug, so I did. Mom knew Josh had ended things, but I'd kept the details sparse, and she didn't know how hard I'd fallen for him.

Although, I guess she was figuring it out now.

"It'll be okay," Mom said. "But you know what you need to feel better?"

Not a lecture, please, Mom. I loved that she was here for me, but her advice sometimes strayed into the pushy territory.

"You need a distraction. Something to look forward to. To keep your mind busy, and off silly boys."

"Mia's throwing a party tomorrow," I offered, and Mom pulled back to look at me with an encouraging smile.

"That'll be fun. And what about your new hobby? Something you can sink your teeth into. Will you be tabletop gaming on Sunday again?"

"I guess I could."

I hadn't spoken to Noah about it, but I could talk to him at Gavin's tutoring tomorrow, before going to Mia's to help with party prep.

"I'll ask."

"I think that's a fantastic idea."

I nodded, then escaped up to my room and collapsed on my bed.

It was possible I fell asleep, because the next thing I knew, my phone was ringing.

Josh. I scrambled for my phone, cursing myself for the hope that flooded through me. Of course it wasn't Josh. But I never would've guessed it'd be Noah.

"Hello?"

"Hello, Allie. It's Noah," he said, as if we hadn't swapped numbers and his name hadn't popped up on my screen.

"Hi, Noah."

Even though Noah seemed fairly relaxed around me now, it seemed odd that he would call.

"Hi. Um, I was just calling because I was wondering if you were free tonight?"

"Tonight?" Was he asking me out?

"Yes, because we're almost at the new moon and the skies

are clear. I'm taking my telescope up to Haven Hill and hoped you might like to join me?"

He was inviting me stargazing? I sat up with interest. I'd always loved the idea of it, but the timing was bad. I didn't want to sit outside in the freezing cold tonight. All I wanted to do was snuggle up with Mr. Giraffe and imagine that things had gone differently with Josh.

Social Allie, the one with the brave face, I'd dig her out tomorrow for the party. She wasn't ready to appear tonight.

"Thanks for the offer. I'd love to go some other time, but I was planning to stay home tonight. I'm not sure if you heard, but Josh and I broke up."

"Oh." Noah paused. "I'm sorry to hear that. But you should come to the bluff. It's rare to have such good visibility. It would be a shame to miss the opportunity."

I hesitated. "I'm not sure I'd be good company."

"Please?"

A smile tugged at my lips from the hope in his voice, and if the idea wasn't so far-fetched, I'd think Mom had put him up to this. Staring out at the universe would be a distraction, a way to put my own problems into perspective.

"You really want me to?"

"Yes, I do. I can pick you up around seven. Is that okay?"

"I'll be ready."

I'd be ready for stargazing. But ready to embrace another new hobby and get over Josh? Not even close.

39

Josh

THE IMAGINATIVELY NAMED Haven Hill was to the south of Haven Valley. It was a nature-lover's paradise. With hikes to suit all fitness levels, and even a small, albeit unimpressive, waterfall, it was a beautiful place to visit. At least in the summer, and during the day. But it was still beautiful out tonight, courtesy of the starlit sky, which was so much more stunning out of town, away from the light pollution.

After driving up the winding road, I parked my car in the small muddy area at the base of the walking trail signposted Devil's Hike. Noah assured me that no one else would stop here, and he'd been right. The people out tonight were continuing up to Point's Bluff.

But not me. I wanted to keep my car hidden, and this was the best way to do it. I intended to surprise Allie, and I hoped it would ultimately be something she'd consider a good surprise.

The hike up took twenty minutes, a little longer than I'd expected, but despite the name, it hadn't been too challenging. I'd relied on the flashlight on my phone to light the way.

The end of the trail opened up into a large clearing. There were a few people already set up with telescopes of varying sizes, but my eyes went straight to the girl camouflaged in the darkness, but still standing out thanks to her wavy blonde hair.

Allie's attention was on Noah as he fiddled with his telescope, but then she switched to staring at the sky.

After a few minutes, Noah said something to her, and she switched places with him, giving her full attention to the telescope as she looked through the eyepiece for the first time.

I drew in a breath. The set-up was perfect—exactly how I'd planned. I approached them with purposeful strides, and as soon as Noah spotted me, he slipped away from Allie and toward me, giving me a conspiratorial nod as we crossed paths. I was going to owe him big time.

"I can't believe the magnification," Allie said, her voice full of awe. "And the star in the middle is so bright. It's incredible."

"That's your star," I said.

Allie tensed at the sound of my voice. Then she cautiously lifted her head from the telescope and turned to face me. "My star?"

I nodded. "Well, you can't technically own stars, but I registered it for you."

Allie kept her eyes on mine as I stepped closer. Other than surprise, her face showed no emotion. "You registered a star for me?" She tilted her head.

I nodded. I wanted to tell her about the stars, but instead my mouth blurted out, "I'm sorry." It was the opposite of the smooth apology I'd been working up to, but it didn't matter. Allie needed to know. "I'm so, so, sorry." I wanted to touch her, to pull her into my arms, but I didn't dare.

"What happened, Josh? I thought that we... I thought that things..."

"I screwed up. And when you said that you—" I stalled, unsure how to even begin explaining myself. I'd been on an emotional roller coaster. I hated all roller coasters, but this type was the worst. "I panicked. All I could think about was how I wasn't good enough for you. How I couldn't give you the relationship you wanted. Because I'm broken, Allie. But I shouldn't have left. I shouldn't have walked out on you. I hate myself for hurting you, and I don't blame you for hating me too, but I—"

"I don't hate you." She gave me a sad half-smile. "I just don't understand. Why would you say you're broken?"

My pulse raced. I wasn't the best at talking about deep feelings, but Allie wanted to know. She deserved to know why I'd tried so hard to resist getting close. Why I'd ended up hurting her.

So I let the words spill out. I told her everything, as best I could, straight from my heart. How I felt rejected by my parents. How they were never there for us when it mattered— or even when it didn't. I told her how hard I fought to protect the few people important to me. It was all I could do. Give them what I never had.

Allie nodded while she listened, without interrupting a single word, while tears gently overflowed from her eyes. She'd watched from the sidelines. She understood. She got me.

"I didn't want to get you mixed up in my issues," I said. "But I couldn't stay away, not when everything between us felt so right."

She smiled, and it was the most beautiful sight.

"I'm so sorry." I'd apologized three hundred times already

tonight, but it would never be enough. "I don't expect you to want me back. But you need to know that what happened was all on me. It wasn't your fault at all, A. You're perfect."

"You don't think I want you back?" she asked, not waiting for an answer. "I love you, Josh."

My heart thumped faster. Those words were so hard to hear. Did she mean them? Was it even possible?

I swallowed. "I love you too."

Allie's face went through a kaleidoscope of emotions. Surprise, disbelief, excitement, anticipation, all bundled together into an expression that manifested itself as a wide, hopeful grin.

"You do?"

"Yeah." I nodded, staring at her with sincerity. "I do."

That was when Allie flung herself into my arms and squeezed me hard enough that all the air left my lungs. I didn't want any distance between us, but I also didn't want broken ribs, so I pried her off.

"Will you give me a second chance?" I asked.

Her actions were screaming yes, but I needed to hear it from her lips.

And her lips were more than capable of answering my question as she lifted her head up to give me a gentle kiss.

Allie was holding back her enthusiasm, and even though I loved it when she got wild on me, this moment was everything I needed it to be. Her lips were cold, but her mouth was warm and inviting.

This was it. She knew everything about me, and she was a force to be reckoned with. She was up to the challenge. She wasn't backing away.

I was getting my second chance, and this time, I didn't plan to ever let go.

40

Allie

THIS KISS WAS EVERYTHING. Despite the biting cold, it warmed my whole body, zapping tingles through to every part of me. Even my fingertips pulsed with heat as I brushed them over Josh's neck.

He cupped my cheeks in his hands, stroking his thumbs back and forth while his lips sent me to heaven. It wasn't the first time he'd touched me with so much tenderness, but after telling me he loved me, and then this? I believed it.

"Wow, Josh," I murmured against his mouth, causing him to pull back with a smile.

His eyes crinkled, and the happiness on his face made my heart melt.

How was this possible?

"Will you show me your star?" he asked. "I haven't seen it yet."

"Yeah, of course." I took his hand—unnecessary, but I didn't care, I had to touch him—and I guided him the single step to the telescope.

Josh ducked down to look through the eyepiece, then after

a second, he pulled back. "Come here. I want to show you something else."

"What am I looking at?" I asked after we swapped over.

Josh wrapped his arms around me from behind, then brought his lips close to my ear. "You see the little star to the right. Four o'clock, close against yours." His breath was hotter than the air, but it still sent excited shivers over me.

"Yes."

He kissed my cheek. "That one's mine."

"You have a star too?" I wanted to turn to look at him, but I was enjoying the feel of his embrace too much.

"It's a binary system. My star orbits yours." His lips moved to my neck, and he placed another gentle kiss against my skin.

"You orbit me?" I asked through a giggle.

"Yes. Always. Or at least for a few more million years." Josh tightened his arms around me. I'd never get enough of this feeling. I felt safe, protected. Loved.

"Don't you get to name the stars when you register them?" I asked, pulling my head away from the telescope.

Josh dropped his arms from around me, then he looked down at the ground, playfully embarrassed.

"Tell me, Josh." I grinned. "What did you call them?"

"Well, you know I'm not the most creative guy." He scratched his head. "So I decided to keep it simple. I called yours *A Star*, because it's your star, A. And because you're the best. Top of the rankings. And because it's a star."

I laughed. That was so bad. "How about yours? J star?"

He shook his head. "That only makes sense one way. For mine, I went with the name that was crying out to be used." He gave me a sheepish smile. I loved this playful side of Josh so much.

226

"Which is…"

He pursed his lips, as if contemplating whether to tell me, but then his smile turned confident. "Josh the Giraffe."

"You didn't." I held in my laughter. "What if I don't want Josh the Giraffe orbiting my awesome star for millions of years?"

He shrugged before breaking out into a full grin. And I couldn't help it. I had to kiss him again.

I WAS SO RIDICULOUSLY high on love it was unreal. I hadn't thought anything could top the feeling from a week ago —the one from before it all went wrong.

But this sensation did. It was like I was floating on clouds. Or maybe soaring on a shooting star.

I tilted my head up, willing the lights in the sky to rocket, but they didn't. "Hey, Noah? What are the chances of seeing a shooting star?"

Noah paused packing up the telescope to look over at me. "Oh, um, shooting stars are actually meteors. The chances are better than you might expect, especially on nights like tonight, but you need to be looking at the right time…"

Josh snuggled me into his arms while Noah talked science, and together we gazed up at the stars while we listened. If something exciting happened up there, I didn't want to miss it. But even if nothing happened, I was content here, happy just being in Josh's embrace.

When Noah was done with his explanation—which had gone slightly off track to explain the different types of space debris—and the telescope was packed into its bag, we walked together back to his car.

"Thanks for all your help," Josh said to Noah. "I never could've pulled off tonight without you."

I nodded to show my appreciation, too. Although tonight had been Josh's idea, getting me out here, and making it possible for us to see our stars—that was all Noah.

He'd left and waited in his car until Josh sent a message for him to join us, something he seemed awkward about at first, like he was crashing our date. But once he started looking through the telescope and pointing out all the sights, it didn't take long for him to relax.

"I'm glad I could help." Noah gave us both a broad smile.

"Well, if I can ever return the favor, you know where to come," Josh told him.

"Thanks, but you've already helped me too."

"I have?"

"Yes. Without you, I never would have put myself out there and tried talking to someone as pr—" Noah stopped talking as his eyes met mine.

"Someone as pretty as Allie?" Josh asked with a chuckle.

Noah gave a bashful nod. He was too cute for words, and my heart desperately wanted him to find the confidence to win over the girl of his dreams, whoever that might be.

"Don't embarrass him," I told Josh as we climbed into Noah's car. He was going to drop us off at the trailhead where Josh parked. "Noah, you know you can talk to anyone, don't you? You're super cute and the girls will love you."

"Thanks, but I'm not very good at talking to girls."

"We can help you."

Josh glanced into the backseat of the car to smile at me. It was as if he could read my mind and knew how much I wanted to play matchmaker.

"Help me?" Noah asked with a level of trepidation which was possibly spot-on for what I was planning.

"Are you free tomorrow night? We're throwing a party, and you should come. I'll introduce you around, and you can practice talking to girls. It'll be fun. I promise."

"Um, thanks, but I can't. Saturday is family night." He sounded almost relieved to have an excuse.

"Come after," Josh said. "Put yourself out there. It'll be worth it."

Noah let out a deep breath, like he was trying to calm himself before something terrifying. "Yes, okay. I'll see what time I can get away."

It felt like a success, but I wouldn't celebrate just yet. Not until he was down in Mia and Josh's basement, surrounded by girls.

Noah dropped us by Josh's car a few minutes later, and after thanking him again for everything, we waved goodbye, and I turned my attention back to the sky.

"Do I need to buy you a telescope?" Josh asked.

I smiled. "No. Tonight's been incredible, but stargazing is a little too arctic for my liking."

I definitely wanted to come back and see our stars again, but I'd prefer it to be a summer activity. On nights like tonight, all I wanted was to stay cozy, snuggled up indoors with my new boyfriend.

"Let's get you somewhere warm." Josh unlocked the car and opened the passenger door for me, but I didn't get in.

"I don't want to leave yet. I want this moment to last forever."

He smiled. "I thought you were cold?"

"I'm not cold when you cuddle me."

Josh laughed, but he took the hint and pulled me back into his embrace. I'd spent most of the evening in his strong arms tonight, and it was my new favorite place to be.

I gazed up at him. "I can't believe this is real."

He answered with a soft kiss.

"What do we do next?" I asked when he pulled back.

"Next?"

"I mean, now that we've already… Do you want to bring back the no-touching rule?"

Please say no. Please say no.

He slid his fingers over my cheek, sending heat searing across it. "I hate that rule, but we can do things however you want."

I grinned, then went in for another kiss, this time letting loose with unabashed excitement. And even though Josh was matching my enthusiasm, I wasn't going to go crazy.

Because this time I already had everything I wanted. I finally had the *real boyfriend* I'd been dreaming of, and I understood what he needed.

He needed enough love that he'd never doubt he deserved it. And I was going to do everything I could to give it to him.

BOOKS BY KENZIE

Summer Expectations

Kisses and Castles (Ava & Colton)

Rumors and Puzzles (Brooke & Tyler)

Haven Valley High

Faking What's Real (Emma & Kai)

Challenging What's Real (Chloe & Nate)

Sharing What's Real (Lauren & Jason)

Celebrating What's Real (Mia & Ryder)

Resisting What's Real (Allie & Josh)

For more information on current and future releases visit
kenziebrayne.com

Plus, get updates and exclusive bonus content when you sign up at
kenziebrayne.com/newsletter

ABOUT THE AUTHOR

A lifelong lover of storytelling, Kenzie originally studied film before turning her attention to the written word. She loves to read and write romance with kind heroes, crushes, awkward moments, temptation, and heart-pounding new experiences.

Made in the USA
Columbia, SC
16 June 2025